Taking Root

a novel

BRENDA BELLINGER

Wordrunner Press
Petaluma, California

Taking Root
© 2020 by Brenda Bellinger

ISBN 978-1-941066-39-3

Library of Congress Control Number: 2020902329

Taking Root is a work of fiction. Names, characters, businesses, places, events, locales, and incidents are either the products of the author's imagination or used in a fictitious manner. Any resemblance to actual persons, living or dead, or actual events is purely coincidental.

Cover design by Stefanie Fontecha

Interior design and layout by Jo-Anne Rosen
Wordrunner Press
www.wordrunner.com

Author photo by movephotography.com

to all who emerge from a dark cocoon

to open their wings in the sunlight

Taking Root

Brenda Bellinger

One

Delaney drops the book she's holding and dives under the circular rack of men's jeans, catching her black Vans tennis shoe on one of the supports. Mostly hidden by swaying legs of denim, she pulls herself into a sitting position on the cold linoleum and covers her ears with her hands. She knows it will be at least ten seconds before the sound of the police siren passes out of earshot.

Peering through the jeans, she sees Betty glance in her direction from the cash register where she is waiting on a customer. The woman, who has been in before, follows Betty's gaze. Delaney scoots further back, watching their interaction, suspecting they're talking about her. She lowers her head and shuts her eyes.

One Mississippi, two Mississippi, three Mississippi . . . Delaney's lips move as she counts silently to herself. At *"eleven Mississippi,"* she crawls out from under the clothing rack, stands and brushes herself off.

Betty removes her glasses, "You okay, hon?"

Delaney nods. Her cheeks flush. Even though she knows Betty has seen her like this before, her heart pounds as she bends over to pick up the sci-fi book she dropped. Shouldering her large camouflage-print hobo bag, she takes a deep breath, turns away and continues to browse.

It's easy for her to spot new inventory since she visits Betty's Bargains a couple of times each week. Everything in the store is donated and well organized: housewares, clothing, furniture, books and jewelry.

Passing by an oval mirror, Delaney catches a glimpse of herself and pauses to smooth her straight, dark brown hair. She wears it parted down the middle with bangs that fall below her eyebrows. She hopes the fringe of thickly applied mascara over her blue eyes, makes her look at least eighteen. Reaching into her huge bag, she applies another layer of frosted plum lip gloss and adjusts the large silvery hoop earrings she bought here last week. She can see why Murray tells her she reminds him of the singer Cher, the way she looked in a '60s poster he has hanging on the wall of his shop.

Below the mirror, Delaney notices a metal platter she hasn't seen before. She picks it up, runs her finger over the wavy pattern along the edge and turns it over. The underside bears a stamped impression indicating it's made of pewter. Betty has a $7 price sticker on it. Delaney hefts the heavy platter for a moment, wondering what it would cost to ship, then tucks it under her arm. She's beginning to feel calmer, that is until she sees a waffle iron like the one her mother had. She sets the platter and book down on a table.

Opening the lid, Delaney remembers how happy she felt the morning her mother, Liz, announced she would make waffles for breakfast. Liz lifted the waffle iron lid, poured batter, closed the lid and walked out of the kitchen.

Delaney waited at the table, humming to herself, her six-year-old feet swinging back and forth as she made patterns with her knife in a tub of margarine. The waffle iron started smoking and Liz returned, cursing. She grabbed the knife away from Delaney, yanked the cord from the outlet and threw the burnt waffles in the sink. Delaney quietly retreated to her room to get away from the smoke-filled kitchen and her mother's rage, with only the empty promise of waffles in her belly.

She closes the lid and turns away at the memory. Picking up the platter, she heads for the jewelry display under the glass counter near the register.

Betty's thick eyeglasses hang from a cord around her neck. She always wears a Betty Boop pin, and today it's fastened to a navy-blue sweater. The image of that character isn't at all like *this* Betty with her plain narrow face and short gray hair.

"Let me know if you want to see anything, hon," Betty says. "Why don't you let me take that heavy platter for you?"

Delaney hands it over, avoiding Betty's smile, and peers through the glass. A new silver bracelet draped over the faded maroon velvet-covered tube catches her eye. The stones appear to be turquoise. The price tag is turned upside down.

Delaney points to the bracelet. "Can you tell me how much that is?"

"The one with the blue stones? Came in yesterday. I don't think the stones are real, but the silver seems genuine. I've marked it at only $8.50 because the clasp is broken. Would you like to see it?"

"Yes, please."

Delaney holds the bracelet in the palm of her hand and then turns it over to look at the back of the settings that contain the stones. On the one nearest the clasp, she notices the worn initials "A.G." She puts the bracelet around her wrist and admires it.

"I'll take this too. Maybe I can fix the clasp." She leaves the tag on the counter and slips the bracelet into her pocket.

Betty rings her up and wraps the platter in newspaper before sliding it into a plastic bag and handing it to Delaney with a warm, grandmotherly smile, "Have a nice day. See you soon."

Delaney steps outside into the afternoon sun and shields her eyes. One of the advantages of living close to downtown is that most of what she needs is within walking distance of her rental unit — a converted garage behind Grass Roots Music. She doesn't have a *legitimate* driver's license or own a car. Her Vans get her where she needs to go. Even though she's lived in Vallejo all her life, Delaney avoids being out alone after dark when she feels most vulnerable. Her confidence sets with the sun. The one time she absolutely needed something at night (tampons), she asked Murray if he'd go with her and he insisted on driving.

Murray is a bit of a loner like her, but he has a kind heart. He agreed to rent her the converted garage behind his music shop at a rate she could afford on the condition she occasionally cover the store if needed (she hasn't had to yet, in almost a year) and that she help keep an eye on his cats, Lyric and Melody.

Grass Roots Music occupies two rooms in the front

half of an older Craftsman-style home on Harrison Street, a couple of blocks off the main street that runs through the old part of town. Murray lives in the back section that has a bedroom, kitchen, bathroom and, sticking out at the rear, a laundry room that must have been added long after the original house was built. Delaney feels safe in her funky little place because Murray is always close by. Often, if she leaves early in the morning, she'll catch a glimpse of him through the kitchen window. She likes the way he looks at that hour before he's had a chance to run a comb through his graying hair. She imagines this is what a father would look like in a home with a normal family.

From the street, with his old VW bug parked in front, her little building looks like a run-of-the-mill single-car garage, it's worn white paint peeling, revealing a grey undercoat. The only door, with a peephole Murray installed for her, is on the side facing his small back yard.

Delaney lets herself in and puts the bag from Betty's Bargains on the table. The overhead garage door that faces the street was nailed shut from the inside before sheetrock was put up to create the interior walls. Except for a little bathroom in the back with a stall shower, sink and toilet, the place is basically one room with a high window on each of the longer walls. The "kitchen" consists of a four-foot section of counter along the back wall, with a microwave on top and half-fridge underneath. Overhead is an open shelf for the few assorted dishes Delaney washes in the bathroom sink. Her furnishings are meager: a futon, an old, pink, give-away dresser, a wobbly six-foot metal utility table, a small bookcase, a computer stand and a steno chair on wheels.

She grabs a can of Diet Coke from the fridge and flops down on the futon. Opening her purse, she takes out her headphones, sets them aside and checks her wallet. Twenty-three dollars and twelve cents. She puts the items back into her purse, finishes her soda and leaves, locking the door behind her.

Delaney turns left at the end of the driveway and takes a short walk uphill to The Office, a mailbox rental and shipping business, to check her mail. She loves her independence and anonymity, particularly the fact that her mother doesn't know where she is. When she first left home, she knew it wasn't likely that her mother would try to find her. She'd wander the streets during the day or hang out in the library if the weather was bad. By late afternoon, she'd find her place in line at the shelter hoping for a meal, a shower and a bunk. Most meals at the shelter were better than any she'd ever had at home. She wasn't sure what put other people off about her — perhaps it was her odd behavior whenever she heard sirens — but the "regulars" at the shelter generally kept their distance, especially the scrawny tattooed guy with the ugly red beard. She got in his face and yelled at him once when he kicked a little black poodle out of his way. A shelter worker told them they both had to leave. Delaney scooped up the whimpering dog, bleeding from the mouth and carried it to a veterinarian's office six blocks away. The dog was thin and dirty and had no collar, but it did have a microchip. When the doctor called the owner, the owner insisted that Delaney wait until she arrived. The woman was so grateful, she paid Delaney $300 in cash on the spot, never knowing that her gesture was what turned Delaney's life around.

Here it is, the middle of July 2000, and twisted red-white-and-blue crepe paper is still taped inside the window frames of The Office. An annoying little chime sounds in the back room when she opens the door. Delaney rummages around in her bag for her keys and unlocks her mailbox. She wishes it were higher, so she wouldn't have to bend over, especially with Alex at the counter.

He looks up from his perch on the stool there, sees her and quickly looks down again. No greeting. Nothing. It's always that way with him. Delaney prefers when Alex's wife, Carol, is working. On those rare days when Delaney wears a skirt and Alex is on duty, she stands to one side of her row of mailboxes, then bends down. There's something about his beady little eyes that gives her the creeps. If it hadn't been for the box number, 201, she would have requested a different one higher up, but this was the month and date of her birth. When Carol first stamped the box number on Delaney's rental agreement, she knew it was meant to be hers. Today, in her baggy, laundry-day jeans, she bends and reaches into the box. Empty, as usual.

Alex doesn't even look up when she walks past the counter to leave. Delaney decides to stop by the store for a few groceries and a package of cat treats; maybe some peanut M&M's for herself. She takes the bracelet out of her pocket and looks at it again in the sunlight. Almost certain the stones are genuine turquoise, she's anxious to do some research on-line to see if she can identify the artist and estimate its value.

Two

L iz takes her hand off the mouse long enough to light a joint as she stares at the screen, waiting for music by the Bee Gees to finish loading. She leans back in her chair and pulls a long drag, remembering the poster of them she had on the wall of her bedroom as a teenager. She'd wanted to tape it to the ceiling over her bed, but her mother wouldn't let her. Liz wonders why she can see the poster clearly in her mind, but she can't picture her mother's face. Maybe it's because she's been dead for 17 years. Exhaling, she watches the smoke rise on an invisible current of air, then carry itself away.

"Spark one for me, would ya?" Jeff says, walking into the living room with a towel around his neck, his hair still wet from the shower. Three months ago, after they'd first met, she envied the way his sandy-blond hair would dry naturally into perfect curls. Jeff's moustache is a couple of shades darker than his hair and it twitches when he becomes impatient. Sitting on the edge of the couch in his jeans, he pulls on his work boots.

"Hey. Didn't you hear me?"

Liz ignores him, hoping he'll just leave her alone. She doesn't want to be bothered. She reaches back, grabs her long, dirty blond hair at the nape of her neck, gives it a twist and piles it on top of her head, holding it there while she sways and sings along to "Too Much Heaven" with her eyes closed.

Jeff mutters something, lifts the lid of the brass bowl on the coffee table and helps himself to her stash. Liz hears the metallic ring when he replaces the lid. She doesn't bother to turn around.

"Stay out of my shit. That's *my* dope. Remember? Get your own." Liz speaks to the screen in front of her as she searches for another song.

Jeff settles himself against the back of the couch, inhales deeply and smiles. "You're cute when you get pissed off, Blondie." He pats his lap. "Why don't you come over here for a minute?"

Liz notches up the volume. ABBA belts out "Dancing Queen."

"Don't you ever get sick of listening to that crap?" Jeff gets up, pulls a wrinkled T-shirt over his head, grabs his dirty baseball cap and heads for the door.

Liz is now out of her chair, dancing to the music in her bathrobe, oblivious to the days' worth of dirty dishes piled in the sink.

"It's no friggin' wonder your daughter ran away. It's almost three o'clock in the afternoon and look at you. Look at this place! When was the last time you even washed your face?"

Jeff leaves, slamming the door behind him. Liz stops dancing, walks to the couch and picks up his damp towel. She stands at the window of the front room and watches his battered red Toyota pickup back down the driveway. She vaguely remembers a time when she used to enjoy the westward view here. From this window on a hillside in Benicia, at the end of a cul-de-sac, she could watch boats on the bay. Lifting the towel to her face, she breathes Jeff in and wonders if they'd ever stood there together to watch a sunset. She can't recall if they had.

Three

Delaney takes the three newest quarters from her woven Guatemalan coin purse, checks them for a "P" mint mark, then drops them into the empty peanut butter jar on her counter. She's noticed that quarters minted in Philadelphia are harder to find out here on the west coast. One of these days she plans to get a set of those cardboard folders for state quarters to begin building an entire collection to sell over the Internet.

Removing the bracelet from her pocket, Delaney lays it next to her keyboard on the computer stand. Someone once told her that Native American artists often sign their jewelry by stamping their initials, usually on the backside. She logs on, types the words "turkwoise bracelet A.G." and lets the search engines do their work. "Did you mean *turquoise*?" her computer asks. She sighs, writes the correct spelling on her note pad, then clicks on the question. Scanning the long list, she doesn't find any links to an "A.G." tied to turquoise bracelets or jewelry. She grabs another Diet Coke from the fridge and sits down to begin researching individual sites for a possible hit, when she hears a familiar scratching at the door and gets up to open it.

"Lyric. How do you always know when I come home with a new package of treats?"

The black and white tuxedo cat meows and rubs his head against Delaney's leg until she strokes his short fur and picks him up. He has a white patch on his chest and white socks on his two front legs. He nuzzles Delaney's chin and makes her sneeze. She sets him down and he immediately jumps on the chair at the computer and paws at the mouse.

"Hey. That's *my* mouse. You leave him alone."

Opening the treats, Delaney removes one, bends over and holds it out until Lyric jumps off the chair. She drops another treat on the floor and reclaims her seat, wondering if she should look up the platter first. Might be easier.

It is. She double checks the mark imprinted on the bottom of the tray in her lap. It's identical to the one shown on her screen. According to an antique dealer on the first website she finds, what she has is an early 19th century pewter tray that could be worth $185 depending on its condition. Delaney jumps up so fast, Lyric runs under the futon for safety.

"Score! Woo-hoo! Hey Lyric, come here you goofy cat. If Betty ever gets new glasses or hires someone who knows what they're doing, I'll have to get a real job."

Delaney checks the pile of boxes under her table to see if she has one that would be the right size. She's proud of the little inventory system she created; empty boxes to the right, boxed items to the left. Every boxed item has a yellow sticky note on it indicating what's inside. One reads "Carnival glass candy dish." Another, "Lionel train caboose." All waiting for buyers. She doesn't have a box that will fit the tray, but she knows where to get one. For now, she sets the tray aside, lures Lyric outside with another treat and shuts the door behind him. As she unwraps a frozen bean and cheese burrito and puts it into the microwave for dinner, a spider crawls up the wall next to the counter.

Delaney has been fascinated with spiders for as long as she can remember. Early on, she'd get as close as she could when she found one, to study its movements. Once, when she was five, she asked her mother why spiders have eight legs. Her mother told her it was so they could run extra fast to catch little girls and bite them. She was relieved when she found out that it wasn't true but remembers being mad that her mother would lie to her. In third grade, she learned how to preserve a web with spray paint and construction paper. Her teacher told the class this was best done outside with adult supervision. Delaney sets her kitchen timer, wondering if her mother will ever be considered a responsible adult.

On the wall over the futon, Delaney has two spider webs that she preserved, displayed; one black on a white background, the other white on black. Both are behind clear plastic in metal frames. Using the edge of her burrito wrapper, and cupping her other hand beneath the spider, she gently flicks it off the wall and onto her hand. She brings her palm up close and makes what she likes to think is eye contact with it for a fraction of a second. The little brown spider scurries around to the top of her hand and she turns her hand over and over, several times until the buzzer goes off. She eases the spider back onto the counter, takes the plate from the microwave and returns to her computer.

After an hour or so of pointing and clicking and countless dead ends, Delaney finally stumbles on a site for a business dealing in "Southwest treasures." It lists numerous Native American jewelry artists by name, unfortunately none with the initials A.G. She puts the bracelet in a small white ceramic bowl on her dresser and checks her online account to see if any offers have been posted for her other items. She's asking $35 for the ballerina music box and has an offer of $25 from someone in Tennessee. By the time she pays for shipping, she'll make less than $20. She takes the music box from under the table and sets it on top. The wooden box is painted light blue. It's in good shape except for a tiny chip in a corner and two barely notice-able scratches on the top but she had mentioned these in her description. When Delaney opens the lid, a miniature blond ballerina with blue eyes twirls to the tune of Swan Lake. One arm is held gracefully over her head and the other, shaped like the handle of a teacup, disappears into the ruffled pink netting of her tutu. Her dance is reflected in the mirrored lid of the box. Delaney watches until the music ends, then reaches under the box and rewinds the key. She closes the lid, sets it back in the cardboard box and responds with the message: "$30 FIRM."

Delaney switches to another site and clicks on music by her favorite band, Whirled Disorder. After getting ready for bed, she removes her headphones from her purse and hangs them on a hook near her pillow. She lies in her pajamas watching the band and recalls the first time she heard WD as a fifteen-year-old.

Her friend Madeline came by in her mother's old Dodge Caravan. They drove over to Blue Rock Park and listened to the new CD Madeline had just bought.

"Check out the lead singer, Dee," Madeline said, pointing to a distorted photo of a scrawny guy on the cover, a studded belt dwarfing the low-slung, torn jeans he was wearing under a black military-style jacket. In the image, his face appeared much larger than the rest of his body, as though he was leaning into the camera. "Is he hot or what? Look at that hair and those chains around his neck!" She turned up the volume. "Just listen to his voice. It's raw."

They'd been parked in the shade, bare feet on the dash, sharing an energy drink when it happened. Again. Back then, Delaney had a pair of worn furry red earmuffs she carried around in her backpack. She'd found them in a clearance bin at an athletic store for $3.99 when she went there with her mother, who wanted to buy that blue thing Suzanne Somers advertised for toning up your inner thighs. At least that's what Delaney's mother told her it was supposed to do. Her mother bought the earmuffs for her even though she told her she thought they were ridiculous for an eight-year-old. When Delaney suddenly reached into her backpack, put them on and then clamped her hands over her ears, Madeline shook her head.

"Dee. You gotta lose this weirdness. Everybody at school thinks you're some kinda freakin' tweaker or something. Dee! Come on. Put those stupid things away!"

Delaney couldn't hear her. She had shut her eyes and was waiting for it to pass. A minute or so later, she opened them and looked around. When she was sure it was safe, she took off her earmuffs and stuffed them back into her backpack.

Madeline turned the key in the ignition. "Let's go. I just remembered I've got a history paper to finish. I'll drop you at home."

"Yeah, okay. Whatever." Delaney avoided eye contact. She reached for the drink and finished it.

Madeline didn't speak to Delaney on the ride back, not even when she dropped her at the curb in front of her house. They still saw each other in classes they shared but didn't hang out together anymore. Delaney had tried to convince herself it was because Madeline had a new boyfriend, but she knew that wasn't the real reason. Still, Madeline had been her only real friend and she missed her.

WD finishes their song. The night swallows the only light in the room when Delaney's computer screen goes black. She pulls the blanket up over her shoulders and waits for sleep to come.

Four

As he closes the blinds over his bedroom window, Murray sees the light from the screen in the studio go out. He can't help thinking about his own daughter who would be twenty-five by now. When he and his wife split ten years ago, she and the daughter took off and headed east to parts unknown. He hasn't heard from either of them since and doesn't expect he will. For three years, he made regular child support payments filtered through the Solano County child support office and then even the bureaucrats left him alone.

Murray hadn't planned to rent out the garage. In fact, when he cut the door on the side and began finishing the interior walls with sheetrock, he thought he'd be using the extra space for storage. Old vinyl LPs were coming back, and folks were bringing dusty armloads into the store hoping he'd offer them some quick cash.

The first time he saw Delaney, about a year ago, she was in the store flipping through vinyl album covers in the "B" section of his new display. That struck him. He couldn't imagine a girl her age would have a turntable. She'd pulled out the only copy of the Beatles' Revolver album he had and was looking at the black and white drawings on the front when she suddenly set it down on top of the others, opened her mammoth bag and pulled out some strange red ear covers that she snapped over her head. They looked like a pair of headphones designed for a cartoon character. She had her back to him, and he remembers standing at the register, watching her carefully. She'd stopped moving and was frozen in position, her hands clasped over the covers on her ears. As he was considering whether to approach her or not, a young black man stepped up and laid a used CD on the counter.

"That girl?" he asked, glancing over his shoulder. "She won't bother nothin'. She's just trippin'. I seen her around before."

"You sure she's okay?" Murray asked in a whisper.

"Yep, you'll see. She'll be fine in a sec."

Murray rang up the sale. The kid took his CD and gave a nod to the girl as he left. A moment later, Murray saw her remove the red thing and return it to her huge purse. He decided to walk over and talk to her.

"That's pretty much a classic, right there," he said, pointing to the Revolver album. "Have you ever heard it?"

"No."

"Would you like to?"

"I can't afford to buy it" she said, having noticed the $15 price sticker.

"That's okay. If you'd like to listen to it for a minute, I'll put it on."

"You have one of those old machines?" she asked.

"Yup, right back here. Follow me and I'll show you."

On a long counter at the back of the room, she saw all sorts of equipment with dials, levers and digital displays in colored lights, along with some speakers and a tangle of power cords. With his sleeve, Murray wiped away a thin layer of dust from the cover of his turntable. Delaney watched as he removed the square plastic cover and pointed out various parts such as the platter and tone arm. Murray carefully slipped the album from its jacket and set it in place. He showed her the needle and explained how it rested in the grooves, then flipped a couple of switches and made some adjustments for sound.

Delaney stood transfixed, watching the album as it spun around and around, and *Eleanor Rigby* poured out of the speaker.

"My sister actually saw these guys in concert back in the late '60s. She still talks about it. John, Paul, George and Ringo. They came over here from England and took this place by storm. Drove the young ladies crazy. Some of them even fainted at concerts."

"Wow, that machine is pretty cool. My mother didn't have one of those. She just had a cassette tape player."

"That's technology for you. Constantly changing. People your age have seen more changes than I've seen in my whole life and I'm over fifty. I don't know how you all keep up with it—computers, cell phones, portable music players—all that stuff."

"Thanks for showing me that. I'd better get going."

"No problem. Come back anytime," Murray said.

She did come back a few days later and Murray noticed she didn't seem to be looking for anything in particular. He recalls wondering if she was a street kid who was a bit lonely. He thought her appearance at the time suggested she may have slept in her clothes — they looked like the same jeans and wrinkled T-shirt she wore the first time she came in. Murray remembers chiding himself for his curiosity about her and writing it off to a rusty paternal instinct.

On the next visit, Delaney told Murray her name when he asked, and he did the same.

"You live around here?"

"Sort of," she replied. "Different places, depending."

He'd pretty much expected that type of answer. What surprised him was his response.

"I'm fixing up an old garage out back. Got some of the sheetrock up and I'll be putting in a little plumbing next. If you hear of anybody looking for a place, you might let me know. It's tiny. Barely big enough for one person. I'm hoping to find someone who won't mind watching the store occasionally and who can help keep an eye on my two cats."

Murray smiles at the memory of her eyes lighting up when he mentioned the cats.

"Okay, I'll let you know," she said and was gone in a flash.

The next day, Delaney was standing outside when he unlocked the front door. He'd barely cleared his throat to offer a "good morning" when she spoke.

"How much are you going to rent your place for?"

Murray leaned against the door frame and folded his arms across his chest. "Well, I haven't decided yet. That probably depends on my finding the right person. I can't rent it for too much anyway since it's really supposed to be a garage. I put a door on the side, so it still looks like a garage from the street. That means it doesn't have its own address or mailbox either. Why, do you know of someone who might be interested?"

"Can I see it?" Delaney asked.

Murray consulted his watch.

"I guess we've got a couple of minutes."

He stepped through the door, turned and locked it behind him, then motioned for her to follow him around the side of the building.

"Here we go." Murray pushed open the newly hung door. "Watch out for nails on the floor."

Delaney stepped into the aroma of freshly cut wood and looked around. Even though it was only half-finished, Murray could see it appealed to her. A fluffy orange and white cat followed them inside and nosed around the sawdust.

"Is this one of your cats?"

"That's Melody. Her brother Lyric is around here somewhere."

Delaney bent over to stroke the cat.

"She's a moody one. Don't let her scratch you."

"Would you rent your room to *me*? I don't have much money right now but as soon as I can get set up in my own place, I'll be able to get some more."

Murray knew he should ask her about her income but decided he just wasn't going to worry about it. Something told him asking about her folks wouldn't be welcome either.

"I guess I should ask you if you're over eighteen."

"Would you like to see my ID?"

"No, that's fine. I trust you. I'm going to need another week or two to get it ready. It might be ready sooner if you want to come over and help on Monday and Tuesday when the store is closed."

"Deal, Murray," she said and offered him her hand. He shook it and that was the first time he'd seen her smile.

Delaney knocked at his back door on Monday morning, before he'd even poured his first cup of coffee. Her purse was over her shoulder and a rolled pink bandana hung from between her teeth as she pulled her hair back into a ponytail.

Murray was surprised at her willingness to work hard. He showed her how to tape the sheetrock and after the mud was dry, she grabbed a roller and gave the walls two coats of cream-colored paint while he installed the bathroom fixtures. He was glad she didn't ask if she could choose her own colors. They worked together for two long, hard days and by late Tuesday night, it was finished. She was vacuuming up the last of the dust when he returned with a pepperoni pizza and a couple of Cokes. Delaney insisted they eat in her "kitchen" even though this meant sitting on the floor at one end of the room. When they were finished, Murray presented her with a key on a black and white lanyard imprinted with musical notes.

"I'll put a microwave and little fridge in tomorrow. Unfortunately, that's going to be it for your cooking facilities. If you find you need an oven on occasion, let me know and you can use mine. You're also welcome to use my washer and dryer, just be sure to take your clothes out when they're done."

Delaney was so excited; she gave Murray a quick hug. "You won't be sorry you're letting me stay here. I'll take good care of this place. I promise."

Other than needing a little help getting her dresser and futon inside, Delaney pretty much kept to herself. She was friendly enough but seemed to enjoy her independence and he respected that. He showed her where she could put her garbage and she'd asked him to pass along any sturdy cardboard boxes he didn't need that could be used for shipping.

Murray never asked about her little business enterprise but two weeks after she moved in, she knocked at his back door and handed him $100. He'd started to wave it away but the look in her eye demanded that he take it and that was how they settled on the charge for rent. Every month since, she paid her rent in full by the end of the first week.

He was carrying a bag of trash outside one afternoon when he saw Delaney standing next to the dumpster, holding a pair of headphones he had discarded earlier. They'd been one of the sets he used in the shop for customers who wanted to preview a CD. The cord became damaged, so he replaced them.

"Can I have these?" Delaney asked. "I mean, if you're throwing them away?"

"Yeah, sure. They don't work though. The cord got screwed up."

"That's okay, they're perfect for me. I love the way they're soft and cushy around my ears and they totally block out sound. Thanks Murray!"

He didn't ask any questions, just gave her a thumbs up and went back inside. The next day when he took the trash out, he saw her funny little red ear-cover-thing sticking out of a bag in the dumpster.

23

Getting ready for bed, Murray remembers that as he stood in front of the dumpster that day, he would have been willing to bet dollars to donuts that his old broken headphones had taken up residence in one very big camouflage-print purse.

Five

It seems the person interested in the ballerina music box has decided they want it badly enough to pay $30. Delaney received an email notification that the deposit has been made to her account, less the payment service's small fee. She pulls the box out from under the table, adds packing material and carefully handprints a shipping label. She likes using the business address for The Office as a return address, believing it gives her some professional credibility.

With the box under her arm, Delaney locks her door and heads up the street to get it mailed. She's in luck. Carol is on duty when she walks in. Her short, perky red hair and brightly colored smocks always seem to liven up the place.

"Hi sweetie. Where's this one goin'?" She reaches for the box Delaney placed on the counter.

Delaney had already stepped away. "Be right back. I'm gonna check my box." As usual, it was empty.

"That'll be foah dollahs and seventy cents and it should arrive in Tennessee by the end of the week," Carol says, in her best imitation of a southern accent. She winks at Delaney and takes a sip of coffee from the happy face mug she keeps behind the counter.

Delaney fishes a $5 bill out of her wallet and quickly checks the design on the quarter when Carol hands her her change.

"Have a nice day," Carol says as Delaney turns toward the door.

Next stop is Bay West Savings and Loan where Delaney uses her ATM card to withdraw some cash from the machine outside. She stuffs the receipt in her purse.

Walking down Main Street, past all the familiar shop windows and vacant lots, she thinks about Murray and how kind he's been to her. He's caring, but in a sort of distant way that she appreciates. She tries to imagine what it would've felt like to have had a father as she was growing up, or even a grandfather for that matter.

Delaney pushes open the door at Betty's, jingling the little bell above. Betty is in her usual spot near the register. Her glasses are perched on the bridge of her nose as her pencil hovers over a newspaper crossword puzzle. The store is quiet, the slight musty smell more noticeable in the cool air of morning. Betty looks up as Delaney approaches the counter.

"Good morning, hon."

"Hi. Excuse me. Do you remember that metal platter I bought?" she asks.

"Yes, dear. I believe I do. Is something wrong with it?"

"No. It's really nice and I've decided to send it to my grandmother. I was wondering if you might have a box I could use for mailing." Delaney flashes her most endearing smile.

Betty turns the folded newspaper over on the counter and sets her pencil on top. A grandmother herself, she's touched by this girl's thoughtfulness and she's delighted to try to be of some help.

"Since it's not busy right now, I'll go take a look in back and see what I've got. Wait here for a moment please."

Delaney walks over to the bookshelf and retrieves the book she'd been looking at the other day, *Perverse Causality*. She sets it on the counter just as Betty reappears with a large, flat cardboard box under her arm.

"Here you go, hon. I think it's about the right size. I found a nice piece of bubble wrap and tucked it inside. I'm sure your grandmother will be very pleased. No charge for the box. That book is fifty cents."

"Awesome. Thanks." Delaney drops five dimes into Betty's hand and slips the book into her purse.

Back at her place, Delaney artfully arranges a white tablecloth on her table, draping the layers of cloth in swirling folds. She peels the price sticker off the platter, places it on top and adjusts an overhead light. She snaps two digital pictures, including a close-up of the imprint on the bottom and uploads the images to her laptop. Satisfied, she puts the platter in the box with the bubble wrap, sticks a Post-it note on the side and stacks it with the others under her table. After folding the tablecloth and putting it away with the camera, Delaney spends the next few minutes writing a brief description of the platter to post with the photos. Considering the weight of the piece and cost of shipping, she sets the price at $220, figuring she can come down to

$200 if she has to. This is the most expensive item she's ever listed for sale and she crosses fingers on both hands as she clicks the "submit" button.

Ready for a treat, Delaney combs her hair, grabs her purse and walks down to The Roasted Bean. Inside, the colors of the walls remind her of summer bleeding into autumn — shades of mustard, pumpkin and a warm, earthy brown. It's almost noon and the place is crowded with people mostly her age or a little older. Some are hunkered over laptop computers; others are reading newspapers and magazines. Couples lean in close to each other, their knees touching. The air is thick with conversation and the smell of freshly brewed coffee. Delaney scans the room and spots the only empty seat - a tall stool at the window counter facing the street, next to a guy who seems pretty absorbed in a book. She orders an iced vanilla chai latte and an oatmeal cookie. Not wanting to disrupt his reading, she quietly perches herself on the stool and begins to peel the plastic wrap away from her cookie. He glances over at her, puts his book down on the counter, slides off the stool and walks back toward the restroom. It almost seems as though he'd been waiting for someone to take the empty stool and keep an eye on his book and cup of coffee, so he could go pee. Taking a bite of her cookie, Delaney discreetly looks over at the cover of his book. It's the *same book* she had just purchased. She pulls her own copy out of her purse, quickly finds her place and begins reading.

When he returns, he can't help but notice her book, the way she's holding it.

"Whaddya think about the story?" he asks, standing next to her.

He tosses his bangs out of the way with a quick jerk of his head and his brown eyes look directly at her.

Delaney sees he's tall, slim and dressed in worn, faded jeans and a pale green striped shirt he wears loose and unbuttoned over a white tee. His dark brown hair almost covers the collar. She guesses he's older than she, maybe twenty.

"I've only just started it. What do you think?"

"I think I want to know what this writer eats for breakfast," he says, taking his seat. "I don't want to spoil it for you. If sci fi and fantasy is your thing, you won't be disappointed. Hey, I don't think I've seen you in here before." He offers his hand and a smile. "I'm Julian, by the way."

"I'm Delaney."

She's surprised at the warmth and firmness of his handshake. At that moment, she hears a train whistle blow and it startles her. Snatching her purse off the counter, she bumps her glass, spilling a little of her drink.

"Sorry. It's my cell." Julian eases his phone out of the rear pocket of his jeans.

Now the train sounds like it's chugging down the tracks until he answers it. He slips off the stool and walks out the front door. Delaney takes a deep breath as she goes to get a napkin, aware her heart is hammering in her chest. Her hand shakes as she picks up her glass to wipe up the mess. She's just settled herself back on the stool with the book when he returns.

"Gotta go," he says as he swallows the last of his coffee. "Hope to see you again, Delaney."

"Yeah. Bye, Julian."

Delaney tries to concentrate on the story but finds she can't. She wonders if he left suddenly because of the phone call or because her reaction to the sound of his ringtone made him nervous and he could use the call as an excuse. It's always like this, she thinks, swirling what's left of the ice around in her glass. In a crowded coffee shop, with music playing in the background, the espresso machine hissing, and people engaged in lively conversation, she feels entirely alone.

Six

L iz drops the towel on the floor and returns to her computer. Her screen has gone dark. Backlit by the afternoon sun slanting through the window, she doesn't recognize the hazy silhouette she sees on the blank screen in front of her. With a long sigh, she gets up and goes to the bathroom. In the harsh fluorescent light, the face in the mirror startles her. She looks like she's sixty rather than thirty-five. Her bleached blond hair is dirty and dull; dark roots plainly visible. Smudged makeup that she can't remember having put on, has left shadows above and below her tired eyes. Her pink terry-cloth robe has unfamiliar stains on the front. Liz looks at her hands and her split and dirty fingernails. She unties her robe and lets it fall to the floor, kicking it aside and stubbing her toe.

Cursing, she steps over the edge of the tub and yanks at the grimy plastic shower curtain. The metal rings screech along the rod above. As soon as Liz turns the knob, the spray of the shower causes an odor of mildew to rise. She begins to cry and leans against the cool tile walls, her body shaking with sobs.

"What's happened to me?" No one hears her empty question. Water and tears run down her body as she lets herself slide to a sitting position in the dirty tub. Steam fills the

bathroom, muffling her cries. When the water temperature begins to cool, Liz pulls herself up. She grabs the bar of soap and furiously scrubs her skin. Shivering in the nearly cold water, she shampoos her hair vigorously, raking her fingernails over her scalp. By the time she finishes rinsing, her body is shaking as she steps out and stands dripping, on the bathroom rug. She reaches for a towel and rubs herself dry, then wraps it tightly around and goes to the bedroom.

Exhausted, she rummages through her dresser drawers until she finds clean panties, a T-shirt and a pair of jeans. Dressed, she slips her bare feet into flip-flops and returns to the bathroom to find her comb and pull it through her tangled hair. Afterward, she brushes her teeth. Twice.

In the kitchen, Liz forces herself to confront the pile of dirty dishes and trash. *"One thing at a time,"* she repeats, over and over, *"one plate at a time, one spoon at a time…"* Her body aches in a familiar way. When she'd finally dragged herself to the public health doctor ages ago, he told her it was something called fibromyalgia. She'd tried all the over-the-counter pain killers, and nothing seemed to work. He quickly looked her over and referred her to a medical marijuana clinic where she was evaluated and given a prescription.

Standing at the sink, scraping off bits of dried food, Liz tries not to think about the pain. *I'm not going to light up until I get these done*, she tells herself as she fills the sink with warm, sudsy water. Her hands remember what they need to do, and she lets her mind drift.

It's been well over a year since she's seen her daughter. Liz has no idea where she is, what she's doing or who she's with. Delaney left not long after she started treating her illness with marijuana. Liz remembers Delaney looking at her accusingly and saying, "Moms aren't supposed to smoke weed. They're supposed to set an example for their kids." Liz recalls slapping her hard across the face for that remark, but she knows that's not why Delaney left.

It was Kirk. He was an idiot, especially when he was drunk. Liz can't recall what she ever saw in him to begin with. He'd had a few beers and grabbed Delaney's ass and then tried to kiss her. Delaney shoved him aside, went to her room, stuffed an old duffel bag with some of her things, grabbed her laptop and walked out. Liz had called after her, but the door slammed shut on her words. Kirk yanked it open and shouted out to Delaney that she was a "stupid little bitch." Delaney just kept on walking and disappeared into the shadows. That was the last time she saw her.

As time passed, Liz found it was easier to just let things be. She pushed her daughter out of her mind and justified this to herself by reasoning that Delaney was almost an adult now and living her own life, wherever that was. Besides, if they were to reconnect and try to repair the relationship, Delaney would no doubt want a lot of things explained. It was too much work. *Too messy. Too many lies to unravel.*

After putting away the last of the dishes, Liz can't seem to muster up the energy to strike a match to light a joint. All she wants to do is sleep and forget. She stumbles into the bedroom, kicks off the flip-flops and climbs into bed fully dressed without even bothering to turn out the light.

She wakes just after 6:30 a.m., to find the light still on and the other side of the bed empty. Jeff hadn't come home after his shift at the warehouse. She throws back her covers and heads for the bathroom. "Men are such assholes," she says aloud.

Remembering the joint she'd promised herself the night before, she lights one up for breakfast, logs on to her computer and finds a video of Michael Jackson singing "*Beat It.*" She closes her eyes and lets herself feel the rhythm of the music as her frustrations and aches begin to ease, just a little bit.

Seven

Delaney marks the page in her book, drops it into her purse and steps outside. At the corner, she crosses the street, checking the front pocket of her jeans for the folded dollar bill she'd tucked away earlier.

Dollar Stretcher has a rack of vegetable plants outside near their double doors. Delaney pauses to look at the limp tomato plants, withering in the heat. She only knows they're tomatoes by the little stakes in the pots. Never having had a garden, she wonders how hard it would be to grow tomatoes. Murray has a hose out back that he uses to wash his car. Maybe he'd be willing to help her find a larger pot and some dirt.

Delaney is holding one of the plants in her hand when she first hears it, off in the distance, the faint but unmistakable cry of a siren. Quickly, she puts it back on the shelf, accidentally knocking another pot over and spilling some dirt. Fumbling, she opens her purse and tries to pull out her bulky headphones, but they're caught on something. The siren is louder. Closer. Dodging customers, carts and kids, she runs into the store in a panic and doesn't stop until she makes it all the way to the dairy section in the back where she clamps her hands over her ears and pushes her back against the cooler. Aware that motion in the store has stopped and people are staring, she's relieved when an employee steps in front of her and blocks their view.

"Are you okay?" he asks.

Delaney takes a deep breath and nods. Looking at the blemishes on his baby-faced cheeks, she guesses him to be barely sixteen. She sees he's sincerely concerned but she realizes she's made him nervous. He quickly glances over his shoulder and then back at her.

"I'll be fine," she says, lowering her hands and trying to regain her composure. "I was just scared for a minute."

"Was someone chasing you?"

"No. It's just something that happens when I hear a certain noise. I'll be okay. Just give me a sec."

He turns to customers watching in the aisle behind him. "She's alright. You can go ahead and shop."

Shopping cart wheels resume their squeaking. Children have lowered their voices.

When he looks back at her, Delaney offers a tentative smile as she brushes some of her bangs to one side.

"Really. I'm okay. Thanks."

He nods and heads toward the front of the store. Delaney tries to appear nonchalant as she walks past customers who avert their eyes. Certain the siren has passed; she goes back outside and chooses the least sad-looking cherry tomato plant. She carries it inside to the bakery section and asks the woman behind the counter to put the largest frosted brownie into a little pink box.

At the register, the young man who'd helped her doesn't even ask if she wants paper or plastic. He puts the pot into a cardboard holder that fits neatly with the bakery box into a paper bag and hands it to Delaney.

Walking home, she thinks about what it would be like to live every day without having to be afraid of her fears — to just be comfortable being who she is — to not have "weirdness" as Madeline put it.

An elderly man who must be stifling under a ratty sport coat and an old wool cap, shuffles toward her. He asks if she can spare some change.

"Here you go," Delaney says, handing him the folded dollar from the pocket of her jeans.

"Thank you, mish," he says, tipping his hat to her and flashing a grin that reveals too many missing teeth. "You're very kine."

Murray is helping a customer when Delaney walks in, so she decides to check her email and return later. Inside her place, she gives the plant some water from the bathroom sink, and puts the box containing the brownie in her little fridge. Wrestling the ice cube tray from a thick layer of frost in her mini freezer, she fixes herself a glass of ice water, then turns on the fan Murray had given her. Next, she pulls her hair into a ponytail to lift it off her sweaty neck.

Logging in, Delaney hopes to find a message with the subject line "Payment Notification." None. She gets up to fix herself a peanut butter and banana sandwich.

Murray is alone when she goes back over half an hour later. He looks up when she walks in.

"Hey. Uh-oh. Only good things come in pink boxes," he says with a grin.

She hands him the box and before he opens it, he asks, "What did I do to deserve this?"

"It's not what you did. It's what I hope you're going to do."

He opens the lid and looks inside. "Holy smokes. With frosting and nuts, even. Whatever it is, I guess I can't say no," he says, lifting the brownie out of the box with its tissue paper. He sets it on the counter then disappears into his kitchen for a minute, returning with a paper plate, knife and two forks.

"This looks too good not to share." Murray cuts the brownie in half on the plate and hands her a fork. "Ladies first."

Delaney takes a bite and smiles. Murray takes a bite and rolls his eyes.

"Okay," he says. "You've got me. What do I have to do?"

"I bought a little cherry tomato plant and I was hoping you might have a container and some dirt I could use. I want to see if I can make it grow."

"That's it? For a brownie this good?"

Delaney nods.

"I think we can figure something out. I'll scout around back as soon as I close. By the way, I'm glad you stopped in. I wanted to talk to you, too."

"About what?" Delaney asks, reaching for another bite.

"I've been meaning to show you some of the things I do here, like how to run the register, handle inventory, those kinds of things in case I need you to cover for me, which I may have to ask you to do sometime soon."

"Are you planning a vacation or something?"

"Not exactly. I wish I could say I was. I've got an older sister in Minneapolis who just found out she's got cancer. They haven't scheduled a surgery date yet but when they do, I want to go back."

"I'm really sorry Murray. I'll help you with whatever you need."

"I knew I could count on you. Are you free tomorrow morning?"

"Sure."

"Come over about 9:30 then so we can have a half-hour before I open."

"I'll be here," Delaney says.

A customer comes in. Murray clears the counter and hands Delaney a napkin. "Thanks for the treat. I'll see if I can find something for your plant a little later and give you a knock."

Delaney nods and lets herself out.

Long shadows are falling across the yard when Murray appears at her door with a very rustic looking wooden planter box; square, about 18 inches tall and the same wide.

"Tell me where you want it and I'll fill it with dirt."

Delaney points to a spot between her door and the rear of the building that always seems to have plenty of afternoon sun and Murray sets it there. He retrieves a shovel from his storage shed and begins to dig up some dirt from under a tree near the back fence.

"It looks pretty tiny in there," Delaney says after they get it planted.

"You know where the hose is. Just keep it watered and I'm sure it'll do fine. I don't have much of a green thumb myself, but I've heard tomatoes are pretty easy to grow."

"Thanks for your help, Murray."

"You betcha. See you in the mornin' hon."

Eight

Delaney pours a bowl of Lucky Charms as she ponders what to wear. Murray always wears shirt and slacks, occasionally jeans. Reaching for a light blue, short-sleeved shirt that buttons up the front and her nicest pair of jeans, she makes a mental note to check the clothing racks at Betty's later. She spends more time than usual on her makeup, adding a hint of blue eye shadow and carefully applying her eyeliner and mascara. Reaching for her strappy brown sandals, she frowns at her toenails. *Damn.* She checks the clock. Her only bottle of nail polish is a shade called Cheeky Pink, but it will have to do. Standing with one foot at a time propped up on her bathroom sink, she paints her toenails and blows them dry with her hairdryer. She inspects her fingernails. Not pretty, but trimmed and clean at least. At 9:25 a.m., Delaney pulls her lanyard over her head, grabs her purse and walks next door.

Murray unlocks the front door and lets her in, the "Closed" sign swinging in the window behind him. He switches on the overhead fluorescent lights.

"Hey, you look nice. Coffee?"

"Oh, sure. A little sugar if you have it. Thanks." Delaney puts her purse on the floor behind the counter.

41

The door to the back hallway is open and Murray vanishes, returning a moment later with two steaming mugs.

"Basically, you just need to worry about opening and closing and ringing up sales, so we'll go over that," Murray says. "I have someone who takes care of my books and pays the bills, so hang onto the mail as it comes each day. You can put it in this box right here," he says, pointing to a metal box under the counter. "Mondays and Tuesdays, the mailman just shoves the mail through the slot. Wednesday through Saturday he comes in and lays it on the counter, picking up anything that I might have going out. You already know the store is open Wednesday through Sunday, ten to six each day. I always try to open five minutes early and close five minutes late. If someone is still browsing at closing time, I don't hustle them out, but I let them know I'm getting ready to close. They usually get the hint. Come over here and I'll show you the machine. It's an older model cash register. Pretty simple to learn."

Murray points out the various transaction buttons and shows her the safe where he keeps the cash drawer. "Always start with a hundred in the drawer, like this," he explains as he counts out the bills and coins in each section and then slides the drawer into place.

"Do you have some scratch paper?" Delaney asks. "I want to take some notes, so I don't forget." She reaches for a pen in the cup near the register as Murray hands her a small note pad.

"If you can hang out here till noon, we can run through some actual sales together and I'll show you how to use the credit/debit gizmo from this side of the counter. Seems most young people just want to swipe their card and go."

"I can stay as long as you like." Delaney glances at the clock. "I'll go ahead and open." She unlocks the door and flips the sign.

Between customers, Murray explains a few other things to Delaney. If anyone comes in with music to sell, she should ask them to come back when he returns. She can log requests for special orders into his spiral notebook, but she should let the customer know the order won't be placed until he gets back. He shows her the paper clock he hangs on the door if he needs to use the bathroom.

"You can put it on five or ten minutes, whatever you need. Be sure to lock the door. You're welcome to use my bathroom in the back. I can see you're a quick study, young lady. We'll do just fine for a week or so with you managing basic day-to-day operations."

Under Murray's eye, Delaney rings up two used Johnny Cash CDs for a customer about Murray's age who seems to be a regular. She takes his twenty-dollar bill, counts back the change correctly and earns a nod of approval from Murray.

"Let me show you something else over here," he says. "As I replace promo posters, I keep the older ones rolled up in this round bin. I label them with the artists' names on the corner, in pencil. You might have a little trouble reading my chicken scratch, though. Don't worry, I do, too. Occasionally, one of the neighborhood kids will come in looking to paper their bedroom wall and I'll let them take a poster or two — no charge. I figure when they get a little jingle in their pocket, they might remember that and come back to buy some music."

"That's nice," Delaney says. "You're sweet."

"Nah. Just good business practice, although my business might be obsolete by then the way technology is progressing. By the way, you'll be doing the parents a favor if you tell the kids to hang the posters up with removable adhesive — you know, the kind that doesn't leave marks on the wall."

Delaney likes the layout of the store; used inventory on one side and new on the other. Murray carries several generations of music media, from resurrected vinyl LPs to cassettes and CDs and even a few eight-track tapes. All are well arranged alphabetically within musical genre.

By noon, Delaney has handled all manner of sales transactions, answered a couple of phone calls, unpacked a shipment of new CDs and priced and stocked some inventory, all under Murray's careful supervision.

"You're doing a fine job here Delaney. What say I wander down to Louie's Deli and pick us up a couple sandwiches?"

"Are you sure you're ready to leave me alone in here?"

"Absolutely. Tell me what you want, how you want it and I'll be back before you realize I'm gone."

"Surprise me!"

Five minutes later, Delaney realizes she should have taken a quick trip to the bathroom before he left. While he's out, the mailman comes by and drops off the mail. Flipping through the small stack, she sees Murray's full name for the first time: Tompkins. Murray Tompkins. She decides it suits him.

Delaney has two customers while he's gone; a young man in a beanie who purchases a rap CD and a middle-aged woman who's just discovered Phil Collins and wants to find a collection of his hits. The next time the door opens, it's Murray.

"Nice to come in that way for a change," he says with a nod.

Sitting on one of the two stools behind the counter, trying not to be conspicuous, Delaney bites into her huge meatball sub and feels a little sauce dribble down her chin. Murray grins and hands her a napkin as he stands to ring up a sale. They take turns eating and waiting on customers.

"Business is always good in the summer. Things will quiet down a bit when the kids go back to school in a few weeks."

"I put your mail in the metal box."

"Tell you what. You've done such a good job, I'm gonna give you the rest of the afternoon off!" Murray pulls his reading glasses out of his shirt pocket, slips them on and reaches for the mail.

Delaney smiles and picks up her purse. "Thanks for lunch, Murray."

"My pleasure. I'll let you know as soon as I find out when I'll be leaving. It'll be a huge weight off my shoulders knowing the store will be in good hands while I'm gone."

Back at her place, Delaney changes her shoes before walking down to Betty's to see if she can find a couple of tops and maybe a nicer pair of pants. When she walks in, she notices a younger woman behind the register whom she hasn't seen before.

Combing through the rack of donated shirts and blouses, Delaney finds two that she wants to try on along with a pair of chinos originally from The Gap. She catches the cashier watching her when she slips behind the flimsy curtain of the so-called fitting room in the middle of the store. A few moments later, she emerges and lays all three items next to the register. Peering through the glass countertop, she asks to see a little antique-looking Y-shaped necklace; an inexpensive piece of costume jewelry. In the fitting room she felt she needed something around her neck with the V-necked top. For less than $35, Delaney walks home feeling as though she's carrying a new career-minded image in her shopping bag.

Nine

Delaney sweeps the concrete walkway in front of her door and looks at the little tomato plant. No longer limp, it appears positively happy to be alive, its little arms outstretched in the morning sun. After giving it a light watering, she goes back inside to wash her breakfast dishes. She promised herself when she first moved in that her place would never look like her mother's. It doesn't matter that she never has any visitors. Dishes done, she gathers up a load of laundry and climbs the steps to Murray's utility room. When she starts the washer, he opens the door from inside the house. Delaney notices his hair isn't combed and he has on a rumpled white T-shirt and faded Oakland A's pajama bottoms.

"Sorry. Hope I didn't wake you," she says.

"Oh no. I'm up. Just trying to find my way to the coffee pot."

"Any word on your sister's surgery yet?" she asks.

"Hopefully, I'll get a call this afternoon. In fact, I'd better get some laundry going myself, so I can be packed and ready to go. Coffee first though."

"I'll set my timer and be back in thirty minutes," Delaney says. "By the way, the tomato plant is looking great!"

Delaney checks her email, then her bank account. Unless you count spam there are no new messages. The low balance in her account is making her a little nervous. Fortunately, she has enough groceries to get her through the next few days and her mailbox rental fee isn't due for two weeks.

When the timer buzzes, Delaney grabs her purse, locks the door behind her and goes over to put her load in the dryer. She has forty-five minutes to make a run down to Repeats, the other thrift store in the neighborhood. She still has a twenty tucked away and maybe with a little luck, she'll find something else she can turn around for more money.

Repeats is a little further away, the lighting inside isn't as good, and the merchandise not as well organized as at Betty's. Delaney pokes around the displays. She wishes she knew something about baseball cards, or coins, or stamps but she doesn't. The young woman at the register calls out to her, "Hey, I like your bag!"

"Thanks."

"No, wait. I mean I *really* like it. I'm into camo and I've never found one big enough for all the crap I carry."

She has short, spiky brown hair and when she steps around the counter, Delaney notices her low-slung cargo pants in a camo print and her black tank top with "RAMPAGE" printed on the front in bold, block letters. She comes right over to Delaney.

"Can I see it for a sec?"

"Sure." Delaney slides it off her shoulder and holds it up for her to see.

"Oh my God, this is *exactly* what I've been looking for. Would you be willing to sell it? I'm totally serious."

"Well, um, yeah. I guess, but I'd need to find another one first."

"Right. Come check these out and see if there's one you like."

Delaney follows her to a table full of purses over near some women's coats and shoes. She looks through the pile. Some are leather; most are made of vinyl or fabric and there are very few shoulder bags. The girl retrieves a couple of purses that had fallen to the floor. She picks up one that's not quite as large as Delaney's but is woven of some sort of natural fiber with vertical stripes in soft earth-tone colors. It has a wide shoulder strap of the same material and closes with a flap that can be secured with a leather loop over a big wooden button. Delaney takes it from her, holds it up and looks inside.

"It's roomy. How much?"

"Are you kidding? Seriously, it's yours. Plus, I want to give you some cash. Twenty okay?" the girl asks over her shoulder as she walks back to the register.

"Twenty? Really? Why don't we just call it even?"

"Because you don't know how long I've looked for a bag *exactly* like yours." The girl takes a twenty-dollar bill from the register and hands it to Delaney.

"You've made my whole day," she says. "I'm Wendy, by the way."

"I'm Delaney. Is this *your* shop?"

"No. It's my mother's. I pretty much get what I want out of here for helping out occasionally."

Delaney moves to one end of the long counter and begins to empty the contents of her old purse into her new one.

"Headphones?" Wendy asks.

"Yeah. It's kind of a personal thing."

"Oh. Sorry."

"It's okay. Here you go," she says, handing Wendy the bag. "Hope you enjoy it." She puts her new purse over her shoulder and looks around for a clock. "Hey, do you know what time it is?"

"Almost ten o'clock."

"Gotta go. Thanks!"

"See ya. Thank *you*, Delaney!"

Delaney is walking quickly up the driveway when she hears the buzzer on the dryer go off. She and Murray almost bump into each other in the laundry room.

"New purse?" he asks.

"I thought it was time for a change. Besides, I think this might be a better look for an almost part-time employee at a music store, don't you think?"

He grins and steps aside, so she can remove her clothes from the dryer.

"Could you come back over for a minute after you drop those off?"

"Yup. Be back in a sec."

When she returns, Murray is cleaning the dryer's lint filter.

"Thought I'd better give you a tour of my living quarters. First, let me warn you. You're about to enter a real, genuine, aging bachelor's pad."

Murray opens the door from the laundry room that leads into his kitchen and with a sweep of his hand, invites Delaney to enter.

Crossing the threshold, she steps onto worn linoleum flooring that appears to be original. The pale blue Formica counter and wooden kitchen cabinets with thick coats of dull white paint and metal handles are definitely retro. The stove and refrigerator are the oldest she's ever seen. There are no dirty dishes in the sink, but everything looks as though it could use a good overall scrubbing. A small wooden table with two chairs sits in the corner. Murray opens and closes some of the cabinet doors.

"You'll find the basics here if you need anything. The key word there is 'basics'."

He leads her into the hallway and points out his bedroom on the left and bathroom on the right. Murray switches on the light in the bathroom and grabs a prescription bottle from the counter.

"Can't forget my blood pressure pills."

Straight ahead is the door to the shop area. As they walk through, Murray opens a door to the right and yanks on a chain to light the overhead bulb.

"I use this closet to store some of the surplus inventory."

He explains how it's arranged and points out a locking cash box that she should use to store the receipts at the end of each day.

"When I go, I'm going to give you a set of keys to the whole works. Feel free to use the kitchen if you'd like. There's a phone in there, too. There's a TV in my bedroom. That's the odd thing about having a store in your house. You give up having a living room and dining room. For the most part, you give up having a life, too. But like they say, it beats the alternative."

The phone rings in the kitchen. As Murray answers it, Delaney gives him a little nod and wave and lets herself out the back door.

She's folding her laundry when she hears a knock. It's Murray. He stands there with his hands in his pockets.

"Ellen is having surgery the day after tomorrow, and it looks like she'll be in the hospital for a couple of days. I've booked a flight out of Oakland at 8:30 tomorrow morning and I need to be there an hour before. Kind of tricky at rush hour but I've arranged a ride. At least this way I'll get there early enough to have some time with her before she goes in. Anyway, here's my extra set of keys," he says.

Delaney takes the large key ring from him and puts it on the hook next to her door.

"I hope she'll be okay."

"I hope so, too. When I know more about how long I'll be needed, I'll give you a call at the store. I've left Ellen's number next to the phone in the kitchen. I'll be staying at her place."

"Okay, Murray. Don't worry about anything here." For the second time, she gives him a hug.

"You're a doll," he says and steps out, closing the door behind him.

Ten

Opening the shop Wednesday morning, Delaney thinks about Murray being airborne, wondering what state he must be flying over at that moment. She's never flown and imagines it might be a little scary at first, but probably nothing like the time Madeline talked her into riding The Demon at Great America with her.

She remembers how good it felt to be able to scream at the top of her lungs because *everyone* was afraid, and they were all screaming, too. Those few seconds the roller coaster rocketed through the corkscrew loop are the only moments she can recall not feeling completely alone with her fears the way she does when she hears the wail of a siren. Turning on the lights in the store, she sends up a silent plea that no sirens pass by while she's working.

Murray told her she'd likely be busy for the first couple of hours after being closed on Monday and Tuesday and he was right. He said folks get restless when they want music but have to wait a couple of days to get it. One of her first customers is a girl in her mid-teens, hurrying to find a Cranberries CD for her mother's birthday. Delaney remembers seeing one in the clearance bin and points her in that direction while she answers the phone. The girl returns a few minutes later with a CD for her mother and one for herself, happy to have found both for less than ten dollars.

The mail arrives at 1 p.m. and Delaney realizes she's getting hungry. Not wanting to lock the store, she waits until it's empty, then runs back to Murray's kitchen where she finds a bruised apple and a piece of string cheese. On the table, she sees an envelope with her name on it. She brings it with her back to the store and tucks it into her purse under the counter. A young man is bent over CDs in the hard rock section.

"If I can help you find anything, just let me know," she says.

He turns around and looks at her.

"Delaney?"

She studies him for a moment. Then it comes to her. The coffee shop. "Julian, right?"

"Yeah. Hey, you work here?"

"Only part-time and only occasionally," she says. She's hesitant to let anyone know that Murray is away and she's alone. The phone rings.

"Excuse me a sec," she says as she picks up the receiver. "Neil Diamond's movie album? Hold on a minute please and I'll check."

By the time she walks around the counter, Julian has flipped through the "D" section in *New CDs* and is holding it up in the air. She smiles and takes it from him.

"*As Time Goes By*? Yes, we have it. It's fourteen ninety-nine. Sure, I'll hold it for you at the counter. We're open till six. You're welcome. Bye."

"What about you?" Delaney asks Julian.

"I'm part of the stage crew at The Petri Dish. Freak Brigade is playing tonight so I've gotta get down there and get to work. Thought I'd stop by here first to see if you have their CD, so I know what I'm in for, but no such luck. Nice to see you though."

"Good to see you, too, Julian. Oh, hey. I finished *Perverse Causality*. Wasn't ready for that ending."

He ducks out the door with a wave as another customer enters.

By six o'clock, Delaney is exhausted. She locks the door, flips the sign and proceeds to count out her cash drawer behind the counter, setting $100 aside for tomorrow. She wraps the register tape around the bills, securing it with a rubber band before putting the money in the locked box in the closet. She knows two things at the end of her first day. She needs a new book to read when it's slow and she needs something to nibble on when she gets hungry. Reaching for her purse, she realizes she forgot to open the envelope. Inside is a handwritten note and five $20 bills:

Delaney,
> *Don't confuse this with the money for the cash drawer. This is for you. Buy yourself some food to keep handy in the kitchen and whatever else you want. Thank you again,*
> *M.*

Her eyes well up. No one has ever been this kind to her before. She puts the bills in her wallet, folds the note and puts it in her pocket. After locking the door to the house, she leaves through the kitchen, remembering to put food and water out for the cats.

Outside, the temperature has eased just enough to be comfortably warm; a lovely evening for a walk while it's still daylight. Delaney wanders down to Dollar Stretcher where she picks up several flavors of yogurt, some fresh fruit, a bag of trail mix with peanuts and chocolate chips, a refillable water bottle, a package of crunchy Cheetos, a couple more frozen dinners and a magazine. On the way out of the store, a pink index card posted on the huge community bulletin board catches her eye. In a feminine script, it reads:

LOST
Turquoise Bracelet
Sentimental Value
Please call

Delaney sets her grocery bag down. She pulls a pen from her purse and writes the phone number on the back of her receipt, making a mental note to call first thing in the morning before she opens the store.

Eleven

The morning sun gives Murray's kitchen a warm glow. Delaney puts snacks away, starts a half pot of coffee and checks the clock on the wall, glad to see it's only a few minutes after 9 o'clock. Anxious to make the call, she pulls the receipt from her pocket and dials the number. After two rings, a woman's voice answers the phone.

"Hi, I hope I'm not calling too early. I saw your note about the lost bracelet," Delaney says, wondering if she spoke too fast.

"Sweet Jesus," the woman replies. "Did you find it?"

"Well, I don't know. I mean - I didn't find it - exactly. I don't even know if this might be the bracelet that you lost."

"Okay now, honey. I think you have me a little bit confused. Did you say you have a turquoise bracelet?" the woman asks.

"Yes, I do. It's turquoise and silver."

"But you say you didn't find it?"

"No. I mean, yes, that's what I said. I bought it at Betty's Bargains a few days ago. It's a nice bracelet but the clasp seems to be broken and I was going to see if I could have it fixed."

"Well. That just might explain how I lost it. One minute it was on my wrist and the next time I looked, it was gone, and I can't even begin to tell you how upset I've been."

"Did you lose it in Vallejo?"

"Why, yes I did. I was over there about two weeks ago visiting my cousin. I took her down to the Dollar Stretcher and that's when I noticed it was missing. In fact, she's the one suggested I post a note there."

"I hope this bracelet is the one that belongs to you," Delaney says.

"Well, here's how we can tell," the woman suggests. "If you turn the bracelet over and look on the back, at one end you'll see two letters kind of stamped into the silver."

"A.G.?"

"Oh, my sweet Lord. Hallelujah! Honey, you just made my day. I can't even tell you how happy I am. I'll come right over and get it. Where can I find you and please tell me your name."

Delaney can hear the excitement in the woman's voice and she's beginning to get excited herself. "My name is Delaney and I have to work until six o'clock. Could we meet after that?"

"You tell me where and that's where I'll be," the woman says.

"Do you know The Roasted Bean coffee shop on Main Street?"

"Yes, I do. How will I know you?"

"I have long dark brown hair and I'm wearing a red shirt and jeans. How will I know you?"

"Well, Delaney, let's make this easy. I'm gonna wear my red straw hat."

"Okay, then. I should be there about twenty after. Wait. What's your name?"

"It's Luella, honey. Luella Mayfield. And I sure am looking forward to meeting you."

Delaney hangs up the phone and glances at the clock. She still has time to run next door and get the bracelet before opening.

~

Business is slower than it was the day before and it makes the day seem to drag on. Delaney has even managed to read her magazine from cover to cover.

At about 2 p.m., Murray calls.

"Hey there Delaney. I like the way you answer the phone. Very professional. How are things going?"

"Everything's fine. Cats are good, too. Got your note and thanks for the money. That was so sweet of you. How is your sister?"

"Her doc said the surgery went very well and she should be able to go home tomorrow. I'm going to stick around and give her a hand for a couple of days and take her in for her check-up on Monday. If everything is okay, I'll fly home Tuesday. Think you can handle it till then?"

"Sure. No problem."

"Thanks, partner. Any mail I need to know about?"

"Not really. I haven't opened anything, but it looks like pretty normal stuff."

"Good. I'll plan on seeing you Tuesday evening then unless I call you otherwise."

"Okay. Take care Murray."

As the afternoon wears on, Delaney finds herself eagerly

anticipating her appointment at the coffee shop.

By 6 p.m., she has the register counted out and everything put away. She flips the sign and locks the front door. In her hurry out the back, she almost trips over Lyric. She scoops up some dry food and fills their dishes before locking the door. Patting her pocket to make sure the bracelet is still there, Delaney hurries down the driveway.

As soon as she turns the corner onto Main Street, she sees a flashing red light several blocks away that appears to be heading in her direction. *Not now!* She stops and fumbles in her purse for the headphones as her heart begins to race. Fitting them over her ears, she looks up to see cars beginning to pull off to the right side of the road. Delaney has two options — duck into a business and wait it out or try to run to the coffee shop two blocks away. The nearest business is the R and R Lounge with its black exterior, pink neon lights and bars on the windows. After that, a vacant lot full of trash, weeds and broken glass.

She breaks into a run, cursing herself for not changing into her Vans, hoping she can make it to the Bean before the ambulance gets any closer. Taking advantage of stalled traffic, she dashes across the street. The ambulance is still a block away. She has half a block to go. Pedestrians hear the rapid click of her heels on the sidewalk and move out of her way. The siren pauses, and the ambulance enters the intersection just as Delaney yanks the door of the coffee shop open and runs inside. She's halfway across the floor before she can come to a stop, aware that everyone is looking at her. Coffee cups are held in midair, conversations have become hushed whispers, the steamer on the espresso machine has even ceased hissing. She stands there, headphones on, her chest heaving as she tries to catch her breath.

Delaney feels a hand on her shoulder, and she turns to see the kindest eyes she has ever seen, looking at her.

"Delaney?"

Delaney nods and tries to speak but can't find any words.

"I'm Luella." Taking Delaney's hand in both of her own, she gently pulls her away from the stares.

"Why don't you come set over here child. I've saved us a place."

Other customers avoid eye contact and resume their chitchat as Luella leads her to a small round table.

Delaney notices Luella's large red hat and suddenly remembers her headphones. She pulls them off and stuffs them in her purse, quickly smoothing her hair with her hands and brushing her sweaty bangs away from her eyes.

"I'm sorry," Delaney starts to say as she perches on the edge of a seat.

"You take a deep breath child, while I get you a cold drink."

Luella goes up to the counter and returns with a large Italian soda flavored with crème de menthe syrup. She puts it in front of Delaney and hands her a straw, then sits down.

"Can you tell me what all that hurry was about?"

Delaney grips her glass and watches as Luella slides her cup of tea to one side and leans in across the table, patiently waiting for an answer, her hands folded. She guesses Luella to be about sixty or so and not very tall. She has a soft roundness about her shape and she's wearing a white cotton blouse with a tiny flower print loosely tucked into a denim skirt. Her skin is the color of milk chocolate. Delaney feels herself begin to relax just a little as she peels the paper from her straw. This time, she doesn't try to fabricate a reason, or avoid the question.

"It's a problem that I've always had," she says, surprised at her honesty.

With a nod, Luella encourages her to continue.

"Did you hear that ambulance go by?"

"I did."

Delaney shifts in her seat and takes a sip of her drink.

"This is wonderful." Delaney tries to force a smile but can't. "I've never had one of these before. I usually get coffee."

"Go on, honey. Tell me about the ambulance."

Delaney lowers her voice as she glances around the café.

"Well, it's not an ambulance, so much. It's the sound of the siren. *Any* siren. I don't know why, but it always freaks me out. I have to cover my ears as soon as I hear one and that's why I always carry headphones in my purse."

"They don't completely block out the sound though, do they?" Luella asks.

"No, they don't. I was running fast because I wanted to get inside here before the siren got closer and louder. Usually I try to get inside someplace, anywhere, away from that noise but when I first heard it coming, I was near a creepy bar, so I decided to try to outrun it."

Luella takes a sip of her tea. The tag hanging over the lip of the little white ceramic pot reads "Earl Grey."

"Can you describe how you feel when you hear a siren?"

"Just afraid. *Really* afraid. My heart beats so fast and even with headphones on, sometimes I have to shut my eyes tight and count to myself until it passes."

Luella sits up straight and crosses her arms. "Hmmm… This sure sounds like a puzzle alright. And you say it's always been this way?"

Delaney takes another long drink and sighs. "Yes. For as long as I can remember. Ever since I was little. Are you a doctor, Luella?"

"What makes you ask that?"

"Your questions, I guess. No one has really asked me about it before."

"No, child. I used to be a social worker in Alameda County before I retired. That's what they paid me to do, pretty much. Ask a lot of questions. Sometimes I have to remind myself I'm not on the clock anymore. Anyway, I didn't mean to intrude."

Delaney reaches into her pocket and pulls out the bracelet.

"It's okay. You made me almost forget why I came," she says with a sheepish grin as she lays the bracelet on the table.

Luella looks down at the bracelet and puts her hand over her heart. "Oh, my Sweet Jesus," she says, picking it up and holding it in her hand, letting her fingers close over it.

"I just can't tell you what this means to me," she says, her voice beginning to break. She fondles the bracelet as though it were a rosary, passing it between her fingers, over and over.

Delaney leans closer and rests her hand on Luella's, for just a moment.

"I'm so glad you were able to get it back."

Lifting a shaky cup, Luella takes another sip of her tea. She looks at Delaney thoughtfully.

"Am I keeping you from something?" she asks.

"No. I don't need to be anywhere."

"May I tell you the story about this bracelet and why I missed it so?"

"Please tell me."

"Well," Luella begins, "When I worked for the County, I was assigned to the Children's Services Division. That meant my caseload was made up of families who were having some kind of trouble. Many of them were poor; some folks had gotten on the wrong side of the law; some came from a long line of family that had difficulty. Anyway, my job was to work with the children and help them find the best way to grow up safe and secure. I often thought that maybe if I could bring a few small blessings into their world, it might make a difference." She paused to drink some tea. "Now, when you work for the government like that, dealing with families, all their stories are confidential, to protect their privacy. So, as I tell you this story, I can't give you any specific details or names."

"Okay, I understand," Delaney said.

"There was this little girl that I'll call Mary. She was referred to me when she was about six years old. Her mother had been heavily involved in drugs and had reached the point where she couldn't take care of herself anymore, much less a small child. Mary's father had left the family. Just gone and disappeared. Mary was often absent from school and when she did show up, she always wore the same dirty clothes. At lunch time, she'd take food away from other children because she was so hungry. Her teacher called the authorities and after they did an investigation, Mary was removed from the home."

"Where did they take her?" Delaney asks.

Luella lifts the tea bag from the pot, gently presses it with her spoon and sets it on her saucer.

"Mary was temporarily placed in foster care while her mother was sent off to a rehab facility. Her mother didn't take to the program and, in fact, was kicked out. Mary couldn't be returned to her, so we had to find a more permanent situation. This took some time because there are special laws for the placement and adoption of Native American children, to preserve their tribal culture. Eventually, Mary was placed with a nice couple who met the necessary requirements to be her foster parents. They knew Mary seemed to have formed a special attachment to me and they encouraged me to visit with her any time. I did this once a week or so at first, then less often later on as she grew older and made her own friends." Luella pauses and glances out the window for a moment.

"What did she look like?" Delaney stirs her drink with her straw.

"She was a beautiful girl. She had dark brown eyes and raven black hair that when it was clean and combed, looked just like pure silk. And her smile, it was the cutest smile I've ever seen. Yes, indeed, she was a precious child."

"When she was little, I would read to her and she was always drawing pictures for me. The last time I saw Mary was after she got her first car; little thing called a Geo. She called me up on the phone and told me all about it, asked if she could come over and take me for a ride. 'Sure,' I said. She picked me up and we rode all around town. Even went for an ice cream." Luella heaves a big sigh and reaches into her purse for a tissue.

"The next day, that poor child was killed," she says, wiping her eyes.

"Oh my God! Was it an accident?"

"It was. She was out driving her car and must have made a wrong turn." Luella pauses to blow her nose. "She wound up in a bad neighborhood where there was a shooting and she was the one that got hit with the bullet. She was killed instantly, right there behind the wheel. I couldn't stop crying about it for days and I still cry when I think about it."

"How horrible! Oh Luella, that's so sad. Was this her bracelet?" Delaney asks.

"No. It wasn't hers. It was a gift from her foster parents to me after Mary's service. The foster mother said it was crafted by her father. Whenever I wear it, I always think of Mary and remember the times we spent together. It's very special to me and first thing tomorrow, I'm going to take it to a jeweler to have the clasp fixed." Luella stuffs the tissue back into her purse. "By the way, didn't you mention that you bought this at a thrift store?"

"Yes, at Betty's, right up the street."

"Please tell me what you paid for it, so I can reimburse you."

"Oh, you don't need to do that. I'm glad I met you and you got it back."

Luella opens her purse. "Delaney, please let me pay you."

"No." Delaney gets up to clear their dishes from the table.

Luella shakes her head and slips the bracelet into a zippered pocket in her purse.

"May I at least give you a ride home?"

"Oh no. That's okay. I live close by and it's still light out. Thank you for the mint soda."

"It was my pleasure," Luella says, getting to her feet. "May I give you a hug?"

Delaney nods and they quickly embrace.

"Thank you again for returning this bracelet. It means so much to me. I'd like for us to get together again. What do you think?"

"I'd like that too. I don't have a cell phone, but I can give you a number where you can leave a message." She writes the number of Grass Roots Music on a napkin and gives it to Luella.

Luella hands Delaney one of her old business cards with the phone number crossed out and her home number written above it. "We'll get together again but, in the meantime, if you need anything, you give me a call, okay?"

"Okay."

They walk out of the coffee shop together and Delaney turns to head up the street by herself, her purse over her shoulder, feeling less alone than she'd ever felt before.

Twelve

Luella can't stop thinking about Delaney as she drives home. Afraid of the sound of a siren her whole life? She figures the girl must be about eighteen. Where's her mother? What caused this to begin with? Why didn't somebody do something? All these questions popped into her mind as she sat there listening to Delaney, but she didn't want to pry. She learned long ago that you have to build a foundation of trust first. Go slow and easy. One step at a time.

Merging onto the freeway to head back toward Oakland, Luella reminds herself to see the jeweler first thing in the morning. Afterward, she'll call Delaney to see if they can arrange to meet again the following week.

Luella unlocks the door to her apartment, flips on the light switch, then tosses her hat and purse on the loveseat. Though small, her one-bedroom flat suits her needs perfectly. She was able to keep most of her maple furniture when she moved in and the neutral champagne carpet doesn't clash with the light blue floral upholstery. Maisey, her Siamese cat, greets her with a long meow and then struts over to her bowl in the kitchen, beckoning with her tail.

"Yes, yes, yes. I know what you want. Just give me a minute you pesky feline."

This is always Maisey's ritual, regardless of the time of day or how long Luella has been gone. As she reaches for the kibble scoop, Luella realizes she's also feeling hungry. While a bowl of leftover pasta warms in the microwave, Luella takes the framed picture of Harold off the bookshelf. His eyes hold hers immediately and she can't help but smile.

"My dear, sweet Harold, I wish you were here. I met the most interesting young lady today."

The microwave beeps. She puts the picture on the table. Sitting down with her dinner, she proceeds to tell Harold all about Delaney and her fear of sirens.

"I know, honey. I know what you're thinking and I'm telling you that the Good Lord brought us together for a reason. I haven't figured that reason out yet but I'm going to be working on it starting tomorrow."

Wiping her mouth with her napkin, she looks at Harold again and shakes her head.

"You just don't worry yourself and enjoy your good long rest. Busy work is a blessing for me. Remember what I've been telling you, I'm biding my time here until the Lord calls me home and you and I will be together again."

Luella returns Harold to the bookshelf, tidies up her kitchen and calls her cousin to let her know the missing bracelet has been found. Afterward, she kicks off her sandals and settles herself on the loveseat to watch Frasier.

"Come on up here girl," she says to Maisey, patting her lap. Maisey hesitates, then leaps up and lays next to Luella where she allows herself to be stroked.

During a commercial break, Luella takes the bracelet out

of her purse and holds it in her hand, looking at it carefully. She closes her eyes and pictures Mary; the way she looked the last time she saw her; the way she'd rolled her eyes and smiled after that first spoonful of rocky road ice cream.

"Mary," she whispers out loud. "Did you have something to do with this? Did you want me to meet Delaney? Do you think I can help her?"

A light breeze gently stirs the wind chimes hanging outside the kitchen window.

"Alright, sweetheart. I'll do what I can." She nods and smiles to herself as she puts the bracelet back in her purse.

Thirteen

Waking up the next morning, Delaney feels a flush of embarrassment rise in her cheeks as she recalls her conversation with Luella. She's never spoken to anyone about her problem with sirens. Not even Madeline. Her mother knew about it, of course, but all she ever did was yell at her or shake her to try and get her to calm down. Luella had been so kind, so attentive and non-judgmental, as though it were perfectly normal to see someone run into a coffee shop in a panic, wearing a set of headphones. The more she thinks about their conversation, the more she realizes she wants to see Luella again and get to know her better.

Delaney showers and dresses early, then goes next door to start a load of laundry before having breakfast. When she comes back, she fixes a bowl of cereal and logs on to check her email. She sees a message with the subject line "Pewter Tray" and her heart skips a beat. The sender is a man in England inquiring whether shipment overseas would be included in the $220 price. Delaney clicks the reply button and types: "I would be happy to ship the tray to you in England for that price. I work with a mailing service and they will be sure it is packed well." She clicks over to some music and does a happy dance as she washes her bowl and straightens up her room.

After moving her load to the dryer, she decides she has enough time to take a quick walk to The Office to check her mailbox. As luck would have it, Alex is on duty. He looks up when she walks in.

"Well, hello. I think you have some mail today," he says as she approaches the counter.

"Can you tell me how much it would cost to send a package to England?" she asks.

"England? My goodness, your little business must be going global," he says with a smirking grin. "Depends on size, weight, how soon you want it to get there. All those little bitty details."

Delaney can't imagine how Carol puts up with him. They seem so different.

"For something this big," she approximates the size of the tray with her hands, "that weighs a couple of pounds. What do think the charge would be?"

Alex looks down at a chart below the clear plastic blotter on his counter and runs his finger down one of the columns.

"Depends on the value of the item. If it's under four hundred dollars, and I'm assuming that it probably is, then it will cost you about twenty-two fifty if you want it sent First Class. Of course, if your measurements are wrong, then the cost goes up. If you want it to get there within a day or two, then it goes way up. It's your call, boss."

"Thanks." Delaney turns away to check her box. There is indeed an envelope inside. It's addressed to "Box Holder" and looks like junk mail sent by some mass marketing company.

She tosses it in the wastebasket next to the copy machine and walks out without giving Alex the satisfaction of eye contact.

At the shop, Delaney's first customer of the day is an elderly gentleman who asks for Murray. He's sharply dressed in a casual polo shirt and slacks, with neatly combed, thick white hair.

"Murray is out right now; may I help you find something?" Delaney asks.

"Perhaps you can. I've recently taken up dancing lessons and I was hoping you might have something by Benny Goodman, so I can practice some of the footwork at home."

"In an album or CD?"

"A CD would be preferable, if you have one."

When she wasn't busy in the store, Delaney had spent quite a bit of time familiarizing herself with the inventory. She promptly locates a copy of Benny Goodman's Greatest Hits on CD and hands it to him.

"My goodness, that was quick," he says. "I don't think Murray himself would have been able to find it that fast. He must be very pleased to have such a capable young lady working with him. I've never known him to turn his store over to anyone else, even when he wasn't feeling well."

"Thanks." Delaney blushes as she hands him his change.

"When he gets back, tell him Al stopped by. He knows who I am."

"I'll do that. Have a nice day!" she says.

Delaney is refilling her coffee cup in the kitchen when she hears the telephone ring. She scoots back to the shop with her cup and manages to pick up the phone by the third ring.

"Grass Roots Music, may I help you?"

"Delaney, is that you?"

She immediately recognizes Luella's soothing voice.

"Oh, Luella. I was just thinking about you this morning."

"Did I catch you at a busy time?"

"No, not at all. Customers seem to come in waves and it's quiet right now."

"I so enjoyed talking with you yesterday, I was wondering if we could meet for lunch."

"I'd really like that. I'm actually managing the store for the next few days, but we could meet on Monday or Tuesday."

"How about Monday, then? I'd be happy to come over and pick you up. Do you like Chinese food? I know a good little place in Vallejo."

"Monday would be great, and I love Chinese food, especially chicken chow mein."

"Where do you live?" Luella asks.

"I live in a small studio next door to Grass Roots." Delaney gave her the address of the music store.

"I'll see you at 12:30 on Monday."

"I'm glad you called, Luella."

Not long after the phone call, Delaney signs for a delivery from UPS, glad Murray had shown her how to barcode and price new CDs. This will keep her busy through the afternoon.

Fourteen

"Are you coming or not?" Jeff yells impatiently, as he holds the front door open.

Liz is wandering around the house, looking for her purse.

"The club is gonna close in twenty minutes and you'll be shit outta luck. I won't be around to listen to you when you fall apart, either. Skip your damn purse. You don't need it. They ought to know you by now." Jeff shifts his weight from one foot to the other.

Liz yells from the bedroom. "They can't give it to me unless I show them my card every damn time. It's some kind of legal deal. Just shut up for a minute and let me think."

She can't remember which purse she used the last time she went out of the house. With the toe of her shoe, she pushes aside a pile of dirty laundry on the bedroom floor. Her purse is underneath. Picking it up, she walks out the front door.

"Get in the goddamn truck," Jeff says. "If you'd get off your lazy ass and clean up the place once in a while you might be able to find your purse. You might even be able to find the damn remote for the TV that's been missing for a week."

Liz climbs in the cab of the truck and closes the door with a slam.

"Just shut up and drive," she says. "I'm tired."

Jeff turns the key in the ignition. "I don't know why in the hell I bother with you, Liz."

"I'll tell you why you bother with me. Because your old lady kicked you out when you lost your job. Do you remember why you lost your job? Because you were a lousy drunk."

Jeff reaches across the cab and backhands her sharply across the face as he brakes to a sudden stop at the bottom of the driveway. She grabs her purse and gets out of the truck.

"Go bother someone else. . ." The door bangs itself shut, clipping off her words as Jeff accelerates and squeals around the corner.

With her hand covering her cheek, Liz makes her way back up the driveway. She goes into the garage and grabs two big, black, plastic trash bags. Letting herself in the house, she leaves one in the living room and takes the other into the bedroom. She proceeds to pick up every item she can find that belongs to Jeff and drop it in the bag — his pillow, his shoes, his dirty underwear and balled-up socks and the few clean clothes he had in the dresser. Yanking his shirts off hangers in the closet, she stuffs them into the bag and pulls it down the hall to the bathroom where she throws in his toothbrush, razor, deodorant and slimy bottle of shampoo. Liz ties the ends of the bag into a double knot and tugs it into the living room.

Opening the second bag, Liz begins picking up his things from other areas of the house including a worn leather jacket, a six pack of beer from the fridge, a half-empty bottle of vodka, an opened bag of fried pork rinds, a stack of unopened mail, a couple of magazines and the rest of a carton of cigarettes. Satisfied, she ties this bag tightly closed and drags both bags out the front door where she pushes them off to the side, under the porch light. Back inside, she rips the lid off a cardboard pizza box that was sitting on the kitchen counter and with a heavy black marker, writes: "TAKE YOUR SHIT. DON'T COME BACK." She props this up on top of the bags where he'll be sure to see it, even in the dark.

Though her face hurts, Liz doesn't stop. She closes and locks the front door, secures the chain lock, then goes through the house to make sure all the windows are locked as well. In the dining room, she puts the stick in the track at the bottom of the sliding glass door and pulls the drapes closed.

In the bathroom, Liz checks herself in the mirror. Her left eye is red, and a bruise is starting to bloom across her cheek. It's tender when she touches it gently. "Asshole," she says to her reflection. "He's just like all the rest of them."

She goes to the kitchen and removes the package of frozen peas from the freezer. These peas have been thawed, refrozen and thawed again so many times over the years, the print on the package has mostly worn away. She wraps it in a dirty kitchen towel and holds it lightly against her cheek as she walks over to turn on the computer. With her other hand on the mouse, she pulls up some music, careful to keep the volume low so she'll be able to hear the sound of a familiar engine if his truck returns.

Fifteen

Delaney is stocking some of the new CDs on Saturday afternoon when a young boy wearing a helmet and carrying a skateboard under his arm, walks in. She guesses him to be about ten.

"My friend told me you have some free band posters in here." He wipes some sweat off his nose with the back of his hand.

"We do! What group are you looking for?" Delaney asks.

"I don't know. My mom finally let me paint one wall in my bedroom electric blue and I thought it would be cool to put some posters up. Can I just look at what you have?"

"Sure. Come over here and I'll show you where they are."

Delaney pulls one of the posters out of the bin.

"Mr. Tompkins writes the name of the band in the corner, like this, but you're probably going to want to unroll each one to take a look at it. Help yourself, but please try to roll them back up neatly when you're done. Oh, and there's a limit of two free posters per customer."

"Okay, cool. Thanks," he said, leaning his skateboard up against the wall and removing his helmet.

Returning to the pile of CDs, Delaney wonders what it would be like to have a mother who lets you do something like paint your room an outrageous color — a mother who would even be willing to have that kind of conversation with you in the first place. The door opens and Julian walks in, saluting her with the cardboard tube he's carrying.

"Hey Delaney, what's up?"

She notices he's wearing a gray T-shirt imprinted with an image of a band.

"Not too much. What about you?"

"I need to know if it would be okay to put up a calendar poster of some of the shows coming up at The Petri Dish. My boss wants me to try to hang some of these at different places around town. I just put one up at the Bean. They were cool with it. Whaddya think? Maybe in the front window?"

The kid shoves a poster back in the bin and walks over to Julian.

"Do you *really* work at The Petri Dish?" he asks.

"Yup. Part of the stage crew. Guess I'm also their PR man now too," he says, winking at Delaney. "You ever been there?" he asks the boy.

"No. My brother goes sometimes. Does that mean you get to meet all the bands?"

"Pretty much. I help set up their equipment, do sound checks, that sort of thing."

"That's awesome!" the kid says. "Could I have one of those posters?"

"I suppose so. Do you promise you'll let your brother and his friends know about the shows?"

"Sure, dude."

Julian unrolls one of the glossy posters and hands it to him.

"Could you sign it for me, so I can show my brother?"

"Be happy to. What's your name?"

Delaney takes a black marker from the drawer and hands it to Julian.

"Hunter."

Julian spreads the poster out on the counter and across the bottom, in a careful script, he writes: "*To Hunter — Nice to meet you. Thanks for spreading the word. Julian, Stagehand.*" He gives the boy a high five and after the ink dries, Delaney carefully rolls it up and secures it with a rubber band.

"Be sure to put it up with removable adhesive so you don't spoil your new paint job," Delaney cautions.

"Thanks a lot!" Hunter says as he starts to dash for the door.

"Hey, wait!" Delaney calls out. "You forgot your ride."

"Duh!" He grabs his skateboard, puts his helmet on his head without fastening it and runs out the door. "Thanks!"

"Well, that's the first time I've been asked for my autograph," Julian says. "Cool kid."

"Murray always saves posters for the kids. I think that's sweet of him. Anyway, back to your question. It'll probably be fine to post your calendar. He'll be back on Tuesday. Would it be okay if I take one and then ask him? He might have someplace in mind where he'd want it to hang."

"Yeah, sure, that's fine. I'll leave this one for you. I've got a couple more to drop off before I go to work so I'd better jam."

"Thanks for coming in, Julian. It was nice of you to give a poster to that kid."

"No problem, Delaney. Good to see you again," he smiles as he closes the door behind him.

Straightening the rolled posters in their bin, Delaney chides herself for allowing her thoughts to return to her mother. Every time her mind goes down that road, she knows it's a dead end. It doesn't matter anymore. She returns to the stack of CDs, reminding herself that she has her own life, her own place, and her own decisions to make. She is careful not to read too much into the smile Julian left her with.

Sixteen

Slumped forward, her chin resting on her chest, Liz has fallen asleep in front of the computer. Music stopped playing long ago and the screen had gone dark. Soft beams from a pair of headlights sweep across the room. Neither the sound of the engine in the stillness of the wee hours, nor the slamming of the truck door wakes her.

Jeff unlocks the front door. When he feels the resistance of the chain, he raises his boot and kicks it open. Startled awake and momentarily disoriented, Liz turns and squints her eyes at his silhouette, backlit by the porch light. She jumps to her feet and is yanked off balance as Jeff grabs her by the hair. Before he can get his hand over her mouth she screams, hoping her voice will carry through the open front door.

"Stupid bitch!" Jeff yells, kicking the door shut behind him.

Liz smells cigarette-laced alcohol on his stale breath. Still holding her by the hair, he grabs her by the back of her jeans with his other hand and throws her face down on the couch. Her forehead hits the armrest. Hard. Knowing he had to have heard the sharp crack of wood from the impact, she lies perfectly still and doesn't make a sound, hoping he'll either stumble off to bed or leave. Her head is pounding but she tries to focus on keeping her breathing shallow. Her mouth is slightly open, and her saliva finds a path along the rolled edge of the vinyl cushion.

Jeff stands over her for a moment, panting, and then drops down heavily at the other end of the couch. She forces herself not to flinch as he sits on her left foot. Her right leg hangs off the edge of the couch at an awkward angle. He puts his head in his hands and begins to whimper.

Liz knows this usually means his alcohol-fueled rage is over. Aware her foot is beginning to throb as well, it takes every effort not to move or cry out from pain. She thinks maybe, if he can believe he's knocked her out, he'll leave. A moment later, she involuntarily stiffens at the wail of a police siren in the distance.

Jeff gets to his feet and staggers out the front door. Liz hears the truck door slam and the engine start. Her hand against her forehead, her left foot tingling, she hobbles to the front window where she stands in the darkness, watching as he backs out of the driveway onto the street. She sees a police cruiser squeal around the corner and come to a sudden stop blocking Jeff's truck. Lights come on in the windows of her neighbors' houses. Two officers cautiously open the doors of their patrol car. She hears Jeff yell at them.

"Move your goddamn car!"

"Step out of the vehicle and put your hands up in the air," commands one of the officers.

Jeff opens his door and steps out. He has trouble keeping his balance as he raises his hands above his head. Both officers approach him. Jeff turns toward the house and yells "You fucking bitch!" As he turns, one of the officers grabs him from behind and shoves him against the side of the truck. The other officer comes around to help restrain him. After Jeff is cuffed and put into the back of the patrol car, Liz sees one of the officers standing near the car, talking on his radio. The other officer comes to the front door. The door is ajar, its latch broken. He glances at the damaged lock.

"You can come in," Liz says, still standing in the darkness. She turns on the overhead light, grimaces at its brightness and raises her hand to shield her eyes.

"I'm Officer Barnes. We had a call from one of your neighbors who said she heard a scream." He glances around the living room and pulls a notepad from his pocket. "I'd like to ask you some questions."

Liz quickly combs her bangs forward with her fingers, then sits on the edge of the couch, her arms tightly crossed over her stomach. She avoids direct eye contact with the officer but steals occasional glimpses at him when he makes notes. The hint of gray in his wavy brown hair leads her to believe he might be in his forties. The gentle way he speaks to her suggests he's at a point in his career midway between cocky arrogance and burnout. Liz complies with his request to take photos of her injuries but refuses medical attention, touching the lump on her forehead gingerly. He also photographs the damage to the door.

"I've got an ice pack in my freezer. I'll be okay."

"Are those bags outside his?" Officer Barnes asks.

"Yeah. Those are his clothes and everything else that belongs to him. I was hoping he would take his stuff and just leave me the hell alone," she says.

"My partner called for a tow truck. The vehicle is being impounded. If you'd like, I can put those bags inside the cab of his truck, and he'll have no reason to come back and bother you again."

"Yes. Please. Is he going to jail?"

"Yes, ma'am. He's being charged with a violation of probation and I'm afraid that's the least of his trouble. I'm going to ask a judge to grant you an emergency protective order for now and I'll leave you with some paperwork about domestic violence. Here's my card. We're going to go book him. You try to get some rest. Do you have somewhere to go or someone who can stay with you?"

"I've called my daughter. She's on her way over." Liz gets up from the couch. "Thanks for your help."

When Officer Barnes leaves, Liz pushes the front door closed and shuts off the light. Standing out of view, she watches through the window as he carries one of the bags down the driveway and sets it on the sidewalk next to his patrol car. He opens it and looks inside. Liz sees him remove the bottle of vodka, open it and pour what is left into the gutter just as the tow truck arrives. He tosses the empty bottle back in the bag and withdraws the six pack of beer. She's surprised to see him hand this to the tow truck driver. Officer Barnes retrieves and inspects the second bag and then stuffs both bags into the cab of Jeff's truck.

After the tow truck driver gets a signature on his clipboard, the patrol car pulls away. Liz watches to see if Jeff will look back toward the house but he doesn't. The tow truck leaves shortly afterward, trailing the old red Toyota behind it.

As she draws the curtains closed, she notices her neighbors' homes have gone dark once again, the only predawn light now coming from the street lamps.

In the bathroom, Liz moistens a washcloth and wipes away some dried blood from a small cut near her right eye. The bruise on her cheek has darkened and the fresh lump over her right eyebrow has begun to discolor. Reaching for her toothbrush, she remembers she hasn't eaten anything and decides there's no point to brushing her teeth.

After unplugging the TV, Liz pulls the TV stand away from the wall and pushes it against the back of the front door. She yanks her pillow and blanket off her bed and lays down on the couch, too sore and exhausted to pick up the thawed bag of peas that had fallen to the floor and return them to the freezer. She closes her eyes but can't sleep. Her head aches and her heart hammers in her chest as though she'd had several cups of coffee. Now she wishes that she'd never talked to the officer. The thought of Jeff being in jail worries her. He'll be so angry about his truck. He hadn't really hurt her that badly. It's just that he drinks a little too much. If only she hadn't screamed.

Seventeen

The jeweler pulls his eyepiece down over his eye and looks at the clasp on the bracelet. "I can have this done for you in a day or two," he tells Luella. "The cost will be fifteen dollars."

"That's just fine," she says. "Whatever it takes. I lost it once and don't want to lose it again."

Luella stuffs her copy of the repair order into her purse and walks down the street to Mother Earth, one of her favorite shops in this part of Oakland. The owner carries a wide variety of fair-trade products and unique items from all over the world. Tibetan prayer flags suspended from the ceiling wave in the breeze when she opens the door. Inside the air is heavy with the smell of South American coffee beans and incense from India.

Turning to the left as she enters, Luella methodically browses clockwise so as not to miss anything. She pauses for a moment at a fountain made of natural rock. The sound of water gently cascading over the rocks into the basin below is as soothing as the soft sitar music wafting through small speakers overhead. Luella is intrigued by the various rocks and minerals set out among the brass figurines, wooden carvings, candles, soaps, scarves and bowls. Working her way toward the back of the store, she notices a display of bracelets made of polished beads from natural stones strung on elastic cords that slip over your hand — no clasp to worry about. They come in a variety of colors. Hanging above them is a chart that explains the metaphysical properties of various gemstones. She spends several minutes looking at this chart trying to identify the corresponding stones in the bracelets. The chart says that rose quartz "promotes the healing of emotional wounds."

Luella isn't sure about that. She believes that wounds, whether they're physical or emotional, are healed by the grace and power of the Lord. But what if a person doesn't have faith, she wonders. She looks at the bracelets and removes one that's made of pale pink stones. She takes it up to the girl at the register.

"Excuse me miss, do you know if these stones are rose quartz?" Luella asks.

"Yes, they are. The stones in that bracelet were cut and polished from rose quartz crystals found in Brazil. That bracelet has great healing energy."

"Did you say *energy?*"

"I did. It's very powerful," the girl says.

"Would you have a gift box for it?"

"No. Sorry. We don't have any boxes, but over there in that basket, we have some little drawstring bags made of different fabrics."

"Go ahead with the next customer," Luella says, stepping aside. "I'll go check those out."

Luella finds a small purple velveteen bag, lined in a pretty shade of pink silk and brings it up to the register.

"Will this be a gift?" the girl asks.

"Yes," Luella says.

The girl removes the price tag, wraps the bracelet in a piece of tissue and tucks it in the little bag.

As she walks back to her car, Luella breathes deeply, then speaks softly.

"Jesus, I sure hope you don't mind having a little help with the healing. I think we're gonna have some work ahead of us."

Her words lift themselves in the light morning air.

On her way home, Luella impulsively decides to stop and have her nails done. This is an indulgence she usually reserves for special occasions. She reasons that having her bracelet back is cause enough for celebration and she's determined to have her hands look nice when it goes back on her wrist.

The young manicurist recognizes Luella when she walks in.

"You have another party?" Mei asks. The last time Luella got her nails done was for the retirement dinner that was given in her honor several months before.

"No, Mei. No party this time," Luella smiles. "I just want my nails to look nice."

"You choose color. I be right back."

Luella goes to the display rack of bottles of nail polish as Mei heads to the back of the shop for a towel and manicure set. She is sitting on the stool at the manicure table when Mei returns.

"I decided to go with a pale, frosted pink this time," Luella says as she puts the bottle on the table.

"Oh yes. Good choice. This one called Rose Quartz. Give you good qi."

"Chee?" Luella asks.

"Like energy," Mei says, smiling. "Soak fingers please."

After her nails dry, Luella heads home to fix herself an early dinner before going to her ministry meeting at the church. She reflects on the day as she heats a bowl of soup and butters an English muffin. It no longer amazes her how one small thing can lead to another. There are no coincidences. Her faith is strong and sure. If you ask her about it, she'll simply tell you that the Lord has her by the hand.

Eighteen

Early Sunday morning, Delaney checks her email to find a message with the subject line "Payment Notification." A deposit of $220, minus the service fee, has been made to her account.

"Yes! Yes, yes, yes!" Delaney hops out of her chair and twirls around the room in her pajamas. She pulls the box containing the pewter platter out from under the table and sets it on top. Removing the platter from the box, she hugs it to herself. "Two months' rent!" She wraps the tray carefully in the bubble wrap and puts it back in the box, securely taping it shut with nylon reinforced tape. Next, she prepares a shipping label with the buyer's address in London. Delaney sets the box aside, telling herself she'll send it first thing tomorrow morning.

This is her last day on duty at Grass Roots before Murray returns. Delaney showers, gets dressed and goes next door early to do some straightening up before opening. Both cats are waiting for her on the back stairs, each claiming its own side of the top step. She scratches their heads and fills their bowls, wondering if they miss Murray, or if all they care about is having food in their dish when they're hungry.

Delaney starts a pot of coffee, grabs the feather duster hanging from a nail by the washing machine and begins dusting some of the shelves in the store. Floating dust motes glint in the rays of morning sun streaming in through the front window. She stops long enough to pop a Backstreet Boys CD in the player. By the time it plays through, both sections of the store have been thoroughly dusted. She'll vacuum the floor and wipe down the counter after closing or do it tomorrow. In the half hour she has left before opening, she quickly cleans Murray's kitchen and bathroom.

As she unlocks the front door and flips the sign, Delaney realizes she's going to miss this daily routine. She refills her coffee cup and puts all of Murray's mail from the metal box on the counter, sorting first by junk versus non-junk and then sorting those two piles neatly by size. She rubber-bands both stacks and returns them to the box as her first customer walks in, a young woman, just a few years older than she. Delaney immediately notices her confident stride and the way she holds herself even as she flips through some of the new CDs. Her auburn colored hair is chin length in front, shorter in back and her clothing is different, too. She's wearing very dressy black slacks and a pale-yellow ribbed turtleneck sweater with short sleeves. Her black patent leather shoulder bag matches her pointed sling-back heels. Delaney wonders if she just stepped out of the pages of a fashion magazine.

"If I can help you find something, let me know," Delaney says.

The woman turns to her. "Thanks love!" she says, with a smile and what sounds like a thick accent.

Delaney can't be sure, based on just those two words, if the woman is British, Irish or Australian. She's never seen anyone who looks like her before and wonders how this woman found her way to Grass Roots Music in Vallejo. She's replacing the roll of register tape in the machine when the woman lays a CD on the counter. The name of the band is Wolfe Creek.

"Are you the owner of the shop?" the woman asks.

"No, I'm not. I just work for him," Delaney replies. She reaches for the CD to ring it up when the woman puts her hand on top of it.

"I don't need to buy it, love. If you were the owner, I was going to introduce myself and thank you for having it on the shelf."

"Oh. Are you a member of the band?" Delaney asks.

"No. My husband and three of his mates make up the group. We're from Sydney, wrapping up a tour of the states. I'm Kate," she says, extending her hand.

"Hi, my name is Delaney." Shaking her hand, she asks "How did you ever wind up in Vallejo?"

"We played in San Francisco last night. Bonza show that was. We have a little gig tonight here in town before we move on to San Jose. One of the guys in the group knows the owner of the hall. You should come if you've nothing better going on. We'll be at The Petri Dish. Do you know the place?"

"I have a friend who works there." Delaney likes the way that sounds — "friend."

"Let me give you a pass." Kate pulls a card from a silver holder in her purse. "Just tell them Kate sent you. Gotta go."

"Hey, thanks!" Delaney says.

Kate helps herself to one of Murray's business cards and waves at Delaney as she walks out. Delaney looks at the CD before putting it back. She can't find a copy in the used section to play. Unrolling the poster that Julian left, she sees Wolfe Creek is billed as "Indie Folk-Rock from Down Under." The show starts at 7:30 so she has plenty of time to get there after closing. Delaney tucks the pass into her pocket.

It's a quiet Sunday, so time passes slowly. At one point, Delaney looks around Murray's place for something to read — anything, even a catalog — but finds nothing. She concludes that some people just aren't readers. Rather than sit at the counter, she methodically flips through the CDs in each section, beginning with "A" in new, to look for misfiles. After she finds a few, she feels it was time well spent.

This had been her slowest sales day yet, so it only takes Delaney a few minutes to count the drawer at the end of the day, paying special attention to the quarters and replacing any minted in Philadelphia with coins of her own. She locks the front door, turns the sign, puts the money away and makes sure the rest of the building is locked before going next door to get ready. She'll finish cleaning up in the morning.

Delaney chooses a bright pink top and short black skirt to wear. She brushes her hair until it shines, touches up her eye makeup and applies a bit of raspberry lip gloss. Adding a pair of black hoop earrings, she hopes she won't have to mess up her hair with her headphones before she gets there.

The warmth of the early evening sun feels good as she walks several blocks toward the old part of town. Even though this area feels run down and outdated, the 'relic' looks of the buildings with construction details from another era intrigue Delaney; things like tiled storefronts, fire escapes and torn, faded awnings. She peeks into the cracked window of what used to be a soda fountain where she can still see remnants of the old countertop and chrome stools with red vinyl cushions. She imagines spinning around on one of those stools between sips of a tall strawberry ice cream soda. Passing by a vacant lot, she wonders what she might find if she went through it with a metal detector.

Delaney takes her place in line and when she hands her pass to the man at the door, he mutters something into his walkie and asks her to step aside. Another young man, wearing the same black Petri polo shirt, appears and asks her to follow him. He leads her into the circular auditorium. As they walk down the aisle, she wonders just how close her seat will be. He shows her to a seat next to a couple of people in the very first row, dead center in front of the stage. Delaney hasn't been inside this building before and she's struck by the towering speakers and racks of lighting overhead. On stage, a technician is checking cords and cables.

"Psst, Julian," Delaney hisses, barely above a whisper. He glances in her direction, smiles and gives her a nod. He's wearing a black T-shirt with "STAFF" stenciled on the back and she notices a radio clipped to his belt. After checking a couple more connections, he hops off the stage in front of her and brushes the knees of his jeans.

"Hey, Delaney. Wow, you look great! See you after the show tonight?"

"Sure. Where will I meet you?"

"I'll have to wrap some of this stuff up. Might take me an hour or so. Let's meet at the Bean," he says.

"Okay, I'll see you there."

Julian disappears around a heavy black curtain to the right as the house lights dim and Wolfe Creek takes the stage to loud cheers and applause. Caught in the edge of the spotlight, her body vibrating from the beat of the base, it isn't long before Delaney is on her feet with the rest of the crowd in the first few rows. She's mesmerized by the haunting drone of an intricately carved didgeridoo and the rhythm of the drums.

It's dark when Delaney leaves The Petri Dish after the show, so she follows a group of people that seem to be heading in the same general direction. The closer she gets to the Bean, the brighter the lighting on the street and the more comfortable she feels. Inside, she orders a medium cup of coffee and an oatmeal raisin cookie and she waits.

Over an hour has passed when Delaney returns the wrinkled copy of the *Times-Herald* to the basket on the floor. The Bean will close at eleven o'clock, ten more minutes. The guy from behind the counter has already begun stacking chairs and sweeping. Annoyed by the irritation she feels, Delaney takes her purse and slips into the restroom. Washing her hands, she thinks about how she'll get home in the dark. Maybe she should ask to use the phone and call for a taxi. It's only a few blocks but she doesn't feel safe walking home alone at this hour. She walks back into the café and finds Julian pouring milk into a cup of coffee to go.

"Hey, Delaney. Sorry I'm late."

He puts his arms around her and gives her a quick hug. She doesn't reciprocate. The owner, whom everyone calls Mrs. Bean, is standing at the door, jingling her keys to get their attention.

"C'mon. Lemme walk you home," he says as they step out into the night. "Matt, the lead singer, asked me to come aboard their bus for a beer after I helped get all their shit loaded. Wolfe Creek is the biggest name band The Petri Dish has ever seen, probably ever will see, so I couldn't say no. Do you forgive me?"

"Yeah," Delaney says, not looking at him.

Julian stops in front of her. "Wait." He puts his hands on her shoulders, but she sighs and looks away. "I mean it, Delaney. I'm really sorry I was late."

Delaney gently shrugs his hands off, steps to the side and continues walking. "I know. It's no big deal. I would have just called a taxi to get home."

"Speaking of that, where do you live anyway?"

"Next door to Grass Roots."

"It was good to see you at the show. How'd you score a front row seat?"

"I met Kate, the wife of one of the band members."

"You gotta love their accents. Everybody's a 'mate'," Julian says.

They walk the next two blocks in silence. When they reach her driveway, Delaney stops.

"So, where's your place?" Julian asks.

"Back there." Delaney tilts her head in the direction of the garage.

"That's a garage. You live in a garage?"

"It used to be a garage. Thanks for walking me back," she says.

"I haven't done my job if I don't get you to your door safely. It's the least I can do."

Delaney had forgotten to leave the light on over her door when she left, so she fumbles in the darkness to insert her key in the lock. She opens the door and flips on the switch inside but doesn't invite Julian in. Standing on her little mat, she looks at him and says "Thanks again. Have a good night."

"You too, mate." Julian leans over and gives her a quick kiss on the cheek. She can't help but smile before stepping inside and closing the door.

Nineteen

Delaney is waiting in front of The Office when Carol unlocks the door at 9:00 a.m. and holds it open for her.

"Were you out catching worms?" Carol asks.

Delaney laughs, puts her package on the counter and checks her mailbox. She's not surprised to find it empty.

Carol measures the length and width of the box with her tape and puts it on the scale. "London, huh? Is the value of the item inside over four hundred dollars? It makes a difference for the cost of shipping."

"No," Delaney says, "It's about half that."

"First Class International will cost you twenty-two dollars and fifty cents but if you want it sent priority, it will be more."

"Oh no. That's cool." Delaney pulls some wrinkled bills out of her change purse and gives Carol the exact amount. "Could I get a receipt, please?"

"Of course," Carol says. "Thanks for always printing your labels so neatly. It helps. You've restored my faith in the younger generation being able to write legibly."

Delaney shrugs and smiles. "One of my teachers really drilled that into us and I guess it stuck."

"Looks like it's going to be another gorgeous day outside

that I'll be missing. Any plans?"

"I've got some work to do this morning and then I'm going to meet a friend for lunch." Friend. There it was again. "Thanks. See ya."

Delaney walks home and immediately sends a message to the buyer of the tray to let him know it's been shipped. Pouring cereal into a bowl, she realizes she doesn't have enough milk and eats it mostly dry, reminding herself to get to the store later.

Outside, she waters her little tomato plant, careful not to get water on the leaves. She's aware that this plant, like Murray's cats, depends on her for survival. She can't wait to show Murray how healthy it is and how much it has grown. Tiny flowers with the promise of tomatoes are beginning to form.

Lyric crouches nearby, licking water dribbling from a small leak in the hose. Delaney hears Melody meowing but doesn't see her. When she turns the water off, she calls her, but she doesn't come. Remembering that she didn't see her last night when she put their food out, she follows the sound of her cries until she finds her, back around the other side of Murray's building. Melody is lying against the cool concrete of the foundation, looking up at her. Delaney bends over to pet her on the head and notices that one of her back legs has a little dried blood on it and appears to be slightly swollen, just above the paw.

"Oh, Melody. What happened to you? Looks like you got yourself into some trouble."

Delaney squats down to get a closer look. She's hesitant to touch that leg and a little worried about picking her up because of Murray's warning about her disposition. Delaney speaks to her softly. Melody's claws flex and she meows as Delaney lifts her gently, carries her inside and lays her on an old rug in Murray's laundry room. She puts a handful of chicken kibble in front of her and dashes inside to grab the phone book. She can hear Melody crunching some food while she flips through the Yellow Pages.

"I don't know if you have a regular doctor, Melody, but don't worry. I'll find somebody to look at your foot." She scans the addresses of veterinary offices. The closest seems to be about seven blocks away. Delaney calls the office and is told she needs to bring the cat in a carrier. When she says she doesn't have a car, the woman tells her they will squeeze Melody in whenever she can get there. She tells Delaney not to feed her and only offer her a few sips of water.

Delaney checks the clock in Murray's kitchen. Almost 10:00 a.m. She decides she'd better call Luella since she doesn't know how long this will take.

She's surprised at the comfort she feels when she hears Luella's soft voice answer the phone. Delaney tells her what happened and says she might be late for lunch.

"Why, honey, I'll just come right over and pick you and that poor cat up. We'll take her together. Do you have a carrier?"

"I'm not sure if Murray does or not. I'm not even sure I know what one would look like."

"Don't trouble yourself then. I have one here for Maisey and I'll bring it with me. I know where Grass Roots is. I can be there in about half an hour. Just give that kitty some love and tell her everything will be fine."

Delaney sighs with relief as she hangs up the phone. She writes down the address of the vet and kneels next to Melody, stroking her head. Melody isn't purring, but she doesn't resist.

Luella swings her old silver Taurus sedan into the driveway and parks behind Murray's VW. Delaney hears a car door close, goes out to greet her and receives a warm hug. Luella is dressed in a pair of navy slacks and a light blue and white striped seersucker shirt. She's not wearing a hat this time and her short Afro-style hair shows just a bit of gray around the hairline.

"You look so nice. I was going to change out of my jeans, but I didn't have a chance."

"That don't bother me and I'm sure it don't bother the cat," Luella says as she retrieves her carrier from the trunk and follows Delaney around to the back of the building. When Luella sets the carrier on the floor near the cat, Melody flattens her ears and hisses at her.

Luella steps back and looks at Delaney. "I'm not sure what that's about but I think I'm going to try to stay out of the way."

"Don't take it personally," Delaney says, grinning. "Murray warned me about her. She gets moody sometimes and will scratch or bite. She tensed when I picked her up and brought her in but then she seemed to relax a little. I'll try to get her in the carrier."

Delaney finds an old, worn bath towel in Murray's linen closet. She folds it, puts it on the floor and gently transfers

Melody to it. As she and the towel are eased into the carrier, Melody emits a low growl, but she doesn't struggle. Delaney latches the metal door shut.

Luella picks the carrier up from behind and takes it outside.

"I'd like to hold that on my lap, if it's okay," Delaney says as she locks the back door.

"I figured you would. Just get yourself buckled in first."

At the veterinarian's office, they enter through the door marked "Cats" and the receptionist gives Delaney a clipboard with a form to complete. She and Luella sit together in the waiting room with the carrier on the floor at Delaney's feet. Melody is letting everyone know she's unhappy while Delaney fills out the form, listing Murray Tompkins as the pet's owner. Finished, she hands the clipboard back to the receptionist who glances over the information.

"Oh. We haven't seen Mr. Tompkins in a while. Are you his daughter?"

"No. I work part-time in his store and I've been taking care of the cats for him while he's away. He'll be back some-time tomorrow." Delaney returns to her seat. Luella reaches over and pats her leg.

The door to the waiting room opens and a tall woman in a white coat asks for Melody. Delaney stands and picks up the carrier.

"I'll just wait for you here," Luella says as she pages through a magazine.

"Hi, I'm Dr. Keegan. Right this way, please." She shows Delaney to an exam room and asks her to put the carrier up on a long stainless-steel table. Delaney notices the doctor's dark rimmed glasses contrast sharply with her light blond hair, which is loosely pulled back into a ponytail.

Tucking a stray strand of hair behind her ear, Dr. Keegan speaks to Melody in a soothing voice as she opens the carrier door, reaches inside and gently lifts her out onto the table. She strokes the cat's head as she turns to Delaney.

"I'm going to give her a mild sedative, so she'll be more relaxed," she said. "Would you be comfortable helping to hold her head still for me?"

"Um, I'm not sure. She's pretty unhappy right now and I don't want her to hate me."

"No problem. My assistant should be free in a minute and she can help us." Dr. Keegan pushes a call button on the wall. "At first glance, that appears to be a bite. I'll be able to look at her leg more closely when she's sedated." She rests her hand lightly on Melody's head.

"Do you mean a bite from another animal?" Delaney asks.

"Yes, usually it's another cat. It's pretty common among cats that spend a significant amount of time outdoors."

At that moment, a cheerful young woman in a brightly colored scrub top enters the exam room. She pulls on a pair of gloves, approaches Melody from behind and gently but firmly holds her head as Delaney moves out of the way.

"It's gonna be okay, Melody. Take it easy."

Dr. Keegan injects a needle into a fold of skin and fur near the back of the neck. The drug works quickly, and Melody relaxes, her meow becoming more of a whispered whimper. Delaney strokes her head while Dr. Keegan examines her left hind leg.

"This definitely looks like a bite that has become infected. Those can be quite painful. Her bones appear to be intact, so we don't need to do an x-ray. I'm going to wash the wound and then lance it to allow it to drain." Dr. Keegan looks at the chart on the counter. "She's an older cat so she's probably beginning to experience some joint pain which is likely why she wasn't up walking on this. Younger cats can sometimes clear these up on their own. If you want to have a seat back in the waiting room, my assistant and I will take care of Melody and I'll give you an update in a little bit."

Delaney returns to her seat next to Luella in the waiting room and begins to tell her what the vet said when she interrupts herself. "Oh, shoot."

"What's the matter, child?"

"I don't know how much this is going to cost." Delaney gets up and goes to the receptionist's window to ask.

"That depends on the procedure and whether Dr. Keegan needs to write a prescription. We should have a better idea in a few minutes," she says. "Melody is one of our patients, so we can bill Mr. Tompkins if you'd like."

"Thanks. That would be great. I'd still like to tell him what to expect though."

"No problem. I'll let you know before you leave."

Several minutes later, Dr. Keegan calls Delaney back in.

"She's going to be fine. It's a good thing you brought her in as soon as you did. I've seen much worse. Her wound has been cleaned and it should heal nicely. I had to give her a bit more sedative, so she'll probably sleep comfortably for the next two to three hours. It's best if you just leave her in the carrier for her nap. While she's sleeping, move her litter box so it's close by. Once she wakes up, let her out to move around. Walking will be good for her. For the next couple of days, try to keep her confined to one room so you can keep an eye on her. If she runs a fever or you see some more swelling or drainage, or any indication she's in pain, let us know."

Dr. Keegan pulls a small bottle of pills from her pocket. "This is an antibiotic in capsule form. She should have one in the morning and one in the evening until they're gone. Open the capsule and mix it into an amount of moist food you can count on her eating."

Delaney puts the pills in her bag, peeks inside the carrier and sees Melody's leg wrapped in a little gauze bandage.

"The bandage can come off in two days if she doesn't pull it off herself before then."

"Thank you, Dr. Keegan." Delaney says, picking up the carrier.

"Be sure to tell Mr. Tompkins we said hello."

On the way out, the receptionist hands Delaney a folded note that reads "$165. We'll mail the bill."

Delaney nods her thanks as Luella opens the door.

Twenty

The telephone rings several times before Liz is jarred awake from her troubled sleep. She winces when she tries to open her left eye and realizes it's still swollen. By the time she gets to her feet and stumbles into the kitchen, the answering machine has picked it up. She hears a female voice leaving a message.

"Hello, Miss Tanner. This is Karen Miller. I'm calling from the Solano County District Attorney's Office. I've reviewed a report from the Benicia Police Department and need to talk to you as soon as possible. Please give me a call at..."

Liz pushes the delete button, noticing the time on the machine reads 11:45 a.m. The bag of peas has left a puddle on the floor. She picks it up and puts it back in the freezer. The TV stand is still pushed up against the front door. Liz wants to move it away, so she can get a better look at the damage. The effort is too much. Her head throbs as she tries pulling on the stand, only managing to move it a few inches. She goes to the bathroom medicine chest to find the bottle of Percocet - a souvenir from one of her former boyfriends. After swallowing two pills with a handful of water from the faucet, she squints at her reflection in the mirror.

Her forehead is black and blue and the oval bruise on her cheek looks worse than it did before. Liz reaches for her jar of foundation and tenderly smears a thick layer on her cheek and forehead, not seeming to notice or care that her eyebrow is plastered down, and she looks like she's wearing a half-mask.

Back in the living room, she sees the chain plate has been ripped out of the door frame by the force of Jeff's kick. The plate and chain hang from the back of the door. The door hinges seem to be okay, but she needs a new heavy-duty door bolt. The only way to get one is for her to get some shoes on and walk down to the hardware store. When she gets back, she can have a joint and figure out how to put the bolt on.

Feeling a little bit woozy, she slides her feet into her flip-flops and tries to steady herself as she pulls a twenty-dollar bill out of her wallet and tucks it into the pocket of her jeans. She drops her keys back into her purse. No need to carry them if she can't lock the door anyway.

Liz squeezes through and closes the front door as much as she can and starts to walk down the driveway. Her feet seem to be moving too fast and the slope of the driveway feels steeper than she remembers. She's curling her toes to try to keep her flip-flops on, but she can't slow down. Suddenly, the asphalt in the street at the bottom of the driveway seems like it's rising up to meet her.

Twenty-One

L uella holds the door open while Delaney brings the cat carrier back inside Murray's laundry room. Lyric follows and Luella gently scoots him out the back door while Delaney freshens up the litter box. Melody is still sleeping soundly.

"Should we go to lunch now?" Delaney asks. "The doctor said she'll probably sleep for another hour or two."

"Won't you worry about her if we're away from here?"

"Yeah, probably." Delaney sighs and her shoulders drop.

"Let's do this. I'll call in an order for Chinese food and go pick it up. If you think your boss wouldn't mind, maybe we can eat it here and keep an eye on her."

"Okay. Good idea. I need a couple of things at the store, so I'll go with you."

"If you can find a kettle, we can have some tea," Luella says as she takes the white cardboard boxes out of the bag. "That's one of the things I like about this take-out. They always include a tea bag with your order."

While the water heats, Delaney sets two places at Murray's small table. Rummaging through his cupboards she finds an old ceramic teapot.

Luella smiles at the mismatched plates and utensils.

"You have to admire a man who doesn't fuss about the style of his kitchenware." She pulls out a chair and sits down.

"I really appreciate your help this morning, Luella. I don't know what I would have done without you." Delaney puts the opened cartons and teapot on the table.

"Honey, it was my pleasure. You know, I think Jesus has a plan mapped out for all of us. Maybe that's why we met, and you had my phone number when you needed some help."

"You sound like someone who goes to church regularly," Delaney says, scooping chicken chow mein onto her plate.

"Yes, I do. In fact, I was there last night for a meeting of my ministry group." Luella lifts the lid on the teapot to see if its ready.

"What's a ministry group?"

"There are different groups for different needs. Mine is called Blessed Beginnings. Our focus is young mothers, particularly young unwed mothers. We do what we can, so their little ones get off to a good start."

"Do you have any children of your own?"

"No. I'm sorry to say I don't. The Good Lord didn't bestow that blessing on Harold and me. Perhaps that's why I've been drawn to children in my work and through my church."

"What does Harold do?"

"He passed on, almost three years ago now. Complications from his diabetes. I truly miss him." Luella pours the fragrant tea into both of their mugs.

"Oh no. I'm sorry, Luella. I shouldn't have asked."

"No need to apologize, child. He was called home before I was, that's all. I'm just biding my time here until it's my turn and we can be together again. What about your folks?"

Delaney pushes her vegetables around on her plate. "I don't know anything about my father, and I don't have any contact with my mother. No brother or sister. No grandparents. So, that's it. I'm pretty much on my own. Excuse me a sec. I'm gonna check on Melody."

A moment later, she returns. "Still asleep."

Luella picks up a bite of sweet and sour pork. "When was the last time you saw or talked to your mother, if you don't mind my asking?"

Delaney shifts in her seat. "Over a year ago. Could you pass the soy sauce please?"

Luella hands her a little foil packet. "Does she live in this area?"

"Benicia."

"Were your parents married?" Luella asks.

Delaney puts her fork down and takes a deep breath. "Once, she told me they were, but I don't know whether to believe her. She lies all the time. It really doesn't make any difference anyway. I guess you either have good parents or you don't."

Luella wipes her mouth. "I'm sorry for intruding, Delaney. I'll hush up. Too many years in my line of work, I suppose."

"It's okay Luella, I don't mind. You're an easy person to talk to. I haven't had someone like that in my life so far."

As they drink their tea, they both hear a faint meow. Delaney goes to the laundry room, kneels by the carrier, unlatches the door, reaches inside and tenderly strokes Melody's head. She sits on the floor and waits to see if Melody will try to come out. Luella watches from her seat at the table.

After a few moments, Melody gingerly stretches and manages to stand up. She shakes her head and takes a few steps out of the carrier on wobbly feet, then settles herself in Delaney's lap.

"Murray told me this one isn't a lap cat. I wish we had a camera," Delaney says.

Luella clears the table and begins to wash the dishes.

"I'll get those, Luella, just leave them."

"That kitty needs you more than the dishes do. Besides, I've always enjoyed warm, sudsy water. Some even say it's therapeutic, so let me be."

A few minutes later, Melody stretches again and lowers herself to the floor. Delaney puts a little canned food in her dish and gives her some water.

"Would you like to see my place?" Delaney asks. "I think the cat will be okay for a few minutes alone."

"I'd enjoy that very much," Luella says.

"Follow me, please." Delaney leads the way out the back door and Luella pulls it shut before Lyric can bound up the steps.

"Is that your little tomato plant?" Luella asks as Delaney puts her key in the lock. "I just love a fresh tomato in the summertime."

"It's my rookie attempt at gardening. Here we are," she says, opening the door. "Except for Murray, you are my very first guest."

"I feel honored," Luella says as she steps inside and looks around. "What a cute place you have Delaney and not an inch of wasted space." Luella sits down on the futon. "Looks like you have all the basics a body would need. You'd never know this was a little unit from the street."

"That's the idea. Murray was originally remodeling it for extra storage space but then he agreed to rent it to me and added the bathroom, the little fridge and the microwave. He's been gone for a week and I've been watching the store for him, so it works out good for both of us."

"What's all this?" Luella asks, pointing to the stacks of boxes under the table. Before Delaney can answer, she holds up her hand. "Nevermind, honey. There I go, poking my nose again where it don't belong."

"Oh, that's just my business stuff. When I find things that might have some value, I advertise them online and if they sell, then I ship them off. That's how I came across your bracelet at Betty's Bargains. I saw it on display and right away I could tell the turquoise and silver were real and that she had it priced super low because of the broken clasp."

"Looks like you have a system to keep everything organized. How do you know how much things are worth?"

"I can get a pretty good idea online. You can find almost all the information you need with just a few clicks and some patience."

"Very resourceful. I'm awfully glad you saw that note I posted at the grocery store," Luella says. "But, like I said, I think we were destined to meet each other. By the way, the jeweler will have that bracelet ready for me tomorrow."

Delaney smiles.

Luella opens her mouth to say something, then closes it again.

"What is it?" Delaney asks.

"Oh, nothing. I think you're a remarkable young lady to have it so together — your own place, your own income, your own life. If I were your mother, I'd be very proud of you."

"Not if you were *my* mother, Luella. I can pretty well guarantee you that right now she's either smoking a joint or getting beat up by the boyfriend of the week. I just couldn't hack it anymore. That's why I left. Between joints and beatings, she sits around in her gross bathrobe and listens to oldies music. Her house is filthy. It's embarrassing."

"Does she know where you live?" Luella asks.

"No and I plan to keep it that way. If she knew I was here she'd probably show up and bring her trash with her."

"Well, I know it's no consolation at all, but I can tell you she's not the only woman in that situation. I've dealt with plenty and it's always the children that suffer. Many women in these relationships have extremely low self-esteem; they're afraid to leave or have nowhere to go if they do and some even think they're to blame for the abuse." She shakes her head. "They always think that things will change, and they don't. It's a sad and vicious cycle."

Luella pushes herself up off the futon. "I should probably let you get back to that cat. You go ahead and keep that carrier for a while in case you need it."

"Thank you so much for coming over here to give us a

ride and for buying lunch. I feel like I've used up most of your day." Delaney opens the door.

"I can't think of a better way to spend my time," Luella says, "I hope we'll be getting together again real soon."

"I hope so too."

After Luella leaves, Delaney goes back to Murray's. Lyric is waiting on the top step, insisting on being let in. When she opens the door, he rushes over to Melody and sniffs her bandage. Delaney lets him visit for a few minutes, then puts him back outside. After sorting the day's mail, she runs the vacuum cleaner through the shop and polishes the glass countertop until it shines. She reflects on Luella's comment about the pride her mother would feel if she saw her. *Never. She'd only be proud of me if I had more bruises or more dope than she does.*

Twenty-Two

Driving back to Oakland, Luella almost misses the onramp to the freeway because she can't get Delaney off her mind. Once she has safely merged into traffic, she offers a prayer.

Dear Lord, I know you put me and Delaney together but I'm going to need some guidance. It's too easy for me to slip into my old shoes and start asking questions like I'm trying to work a case that's been handed to me. But wait a minute here, I guess that's what you did, isn't it? Maybe you're trying to tell me I wasn't ready to retire yet. Well, shoot. If that's your message, then I surely missed it earlier. Can't go back now though. They filled my position. What I'm going to need your help with, is this. I want to get to the bottom of the siren fear this girl has and hopefully help her overcome it. Now I've only been with her a couple of times, but my read is that she's a young woman with a whole lot of promise. She just needs to get over this big hurdle. Living where she does, I imagine she has to deal with that at least a couple times a day. One more thing while I have your ear, please. Help me to find at least someone with a family connection to her who cares, and I understand that's not likely to be her mother. In the name of Jesus, I thank you for listening and for your patience with me. Everyday. And thank you for keeping care of Harold and Mary.

Luella decides to stop by the jewelry store to see if her bracelet is ready.

"This is a lovely bracelet, ma'am," the jeweler says. "I've replaced the clasp and polished it up a bit. Would you like to wear it?"

"I surely would." Luella offers her wrist and he fastens it for her. "It's a special bracelet that holds a lot of meaning for me. Thank you for fixing it. You've done a fine job."

By the time she reaches her apartment, Luella has formulated a plan. Letting herself in, she bends down to pet Maisey, but the cat moves just out of reach with a dismissive wave of her tail.

"And Delaney thinks she's got a moody one. Wait till she meets you, sister."

Luella settles herself at the table for a face-to-face with Harold. With the tip of her finger, she traces the outline of his cheek in the photograph as she tells him what she's learned about Delaney and what she plans to do.

"No. I didn't give her the rose quartz bracelet yet. It's not the right time. We'll be getting together again soon. I'm treading lightly here, Harold. The girl needs help and before I can help her, she has to trust me. That doesn't happen overnight, so you need to be patient. I'm going to give her a call in a day or so and we'll take it from there. Don't you worry, I'll keep you in the loop. In fact, I think I'm going to bring her over here to see my place and meet this finicky feline."

Twenty-Three

Murray returns Tuesday afternoon to find his back door unlocked and Delaney sitting on the floor of the laundry room with Melody in her lap.

"Well, look at this. If you'd told me she'd gotten up on your lap, I wouldn't have believed it."

At the sound of his voice, Melody lifts herself with her front legs and meows.

"Hey there, Gimpy. What happened to you?"

She pushes her head against his hand as he scratches her behind the ears.

"It's good to see you Murray. I'm glad you're back. Somehow, she got bit by another cat and had an infection. She needs to take medication twice a day. I'm afraid you're going to be getting a bill for a hundred and sixty-five dollars from Dr. Keegan. I hope it's okay that I took her in," Delaney says.

"Of course, that's fine, but how did you manage? I didn't leave you the name or number for the vet. I should have."

"I just looked for the closest one in your old phone book. Turns out it was the right place."

"Did you find my cat carrier?"

"A friend of mine brought hers and drove me over. Melody was really good even though I'm sure her leg must have hurt like heck. I've been keeping a close eye on her."

Delaney eases Melody off her lap and stands as Lyric races up the steps wanting some attention, too. He rubs himself against Murray's leg and purrs.

"There's quite a bit of mail for you to go through but I've separated it into junk and not junk. I left some cans of cat food on the kitchen counter. I'll come over later to feed her if you want and show you what to do with the pills."

"How about you come over later and I spring for a pizza? I'll go through the mail and get some laundry started first. See you about six thirty?"

"Okay. Thanks Murray."

Delaney takes advantage of the time to run some errands. She decides to start with a visit to the bookshelf at Repeats.

Wendy recognizes her when she walks in.

"Hey girl, what's up?" she asks.

Before Delaney can answer, she hears the shriek of a siren. It is so sudden, so piercing and so loud, it seems as though it's right outside. Trembling, she can't get her purse open. She panics and puts her hands over her ears and screams, trying to drown out the sound. Wendy, startled, puts her hands over her ears and stares at Delaney, not sure what to do. Wendy's mother comes running from the room at the back of the store.

"Girls! What in heaven is the matter?"

By then, the emergency vehicle, whatever it was, has moved away and the sound of the siren is beginning to fade.

"I don't know, Mom," Wendy says, dropping her hands. "Hey. Are you okay?" she asks Delaney.

Delaney takes her hands away from her ears and tries to apologize but winds up in tears. Wendy's mother grabs a box of tissues from behind the counter and offers them to her.

"Oh my God, I'm sorry. This is so embarrassing." Delaney's hand is shaking as she reaches for a tissue.

"Hey, it's okay. Really." Wendy pats her shoulder gently.

"I don't know what it is. The sound of a siren terrifies me, and it's been that way for as long as I can remember. I couldn't get the headphones out of my purse fast enough. It sounded so close and I didn't know what to do, so I screamed to try to drown it out. Look." She reaches inside her purse and pulls out the headphones.

"If I hear a siren coming from the distance and I have time to put these on, then I can get through it," Delaney says. "This one seemed to start up out of nowhere and it caught me totally off guard. I'm sorry about screaming. That noise freaks me out."

"It's alright, dear," Wendy's mother says, grateful no other customers were in the store just then. "Everyone has things that they're afraid of. It's snakes, for me. That's why I could never live in the country and I don't like to go on hikes. Now that you've got my adrenalin going, I can go back to what I was doing feeling re-energized." She gives Delaney a warm smile. "Holler if you need me, I'll be in the back. Sorry. Poor choice of words."

Delaney looks at Wendy. "I'm sorry if I scared you. God, it's so embarrassing. I hate when that happens."

Wendy shrugs. "No worries. Seriously, I mean it."

Delaney stuffs her headphones back into her purse.

"Thanks. Phew. I came by to see if you had any new sci-fi books."

"We might have a few. Some guy brought in a big box of paperbacks the other day, but I haven't gone through them yet. Wanna help me sort them?"

"Sure, it's the least I can do after almost giving your mother a heart attack."

Wendy drags the box over to the book section while Delaney straightens up books already on the shelves, to make more space.

"That's horrible," Wendy says, "to have panic attacks like that and not know what you can do about it. Didn't your mom ever try to get it figured it out?"

"No. Do you want me to move the little kids' books to the bottom two shelves, so they can reach them?"

"Oh, yeah. Good idea. That was a quick change of subject. I'm guessing you don't want to talk about your mom."

"Right."

After about twenty minutes, the books are sorted, and the shelves are reorganized. Delaney chooses two paperbacks in good condition.

"Those are on the house. A small token of appreciation for your help. Come by anytime."

"Thanks, Wendy, I will."

At the Dollar Stretcher, Delaney buys a full bag of groceries, including a box of jasmine tea bags. She'd enjoyed the tea with Luella yesterday afternoon and thinks she might just start nuking a cup of water once in a while to make her own. On the way out, she stops at the community bulletin board and removes Luella's notice, slipping it into her pocket.

After putting her groceries away, Delaney knocks at Murray's back door.

"Come in," he says. "Your timing is impeccable my dear. The pizza has just arrived."

Delaney notices the kitchen table is set for two. "I brought dessert," she says and hands him a little pink box.

"Well, you shouldn't have, but I'm glad you did." Murray grins.

As they eat their pizza with a dryer load tumbling in the background, Delaney fills Murray in on shop business while he was away. She tells him someone named Al had stopped in to see him.

"He's an old buddy of mine. We go way back."

Delaney asks how Ellen is doing. Murray tells her about the surgery and what he'd done around Ellen's place to make it a little easier for her to recuperate.

"You did such a fine job covering for me," he says, "I'm already thinking I might go back and visit her again over the holidays."

"That's fine with me, Murray. On Sunday, I was beginning to realize I was going to miss the routine over here when you came back."

"Well, maybe we can work a deal where you help out on a more regular basis if you really enjoy it. You did a great job with the daily receipts and balancing the drawer, too. Must have had an easy time with math in school. I found your notes on those special orders and I'll take care of them first thing in the morning."

Melody is limping around her empty food dish. Delaney gets up and first puts some dry food in Lyric's dish outside and closes the door. Then she opens a can of cat food, shakes one capsule out of the pill bottle, opens it, stirs the contents into the food then spoons the food into Melody's dish.

"No wonder she sits on your lap," Murray says. "You're spoiling her with that canned stuff. She never gets giblets and gravy from me."

"That's why I've been feeding him first, so he doesn't get jealous."

"Coffee?" Murray asks.

"Sure. Thanks."

Murray flips the switch on the pot. He rustles around in a paper bag and then in the sink for a few minutes. He sets the pink box on the table and opens it. Inside this time are two macaroons, dipped in dark chocolate.

"You're spoiling me, too!" He pours coffee into two identical green ceramic mugs that Delaney doesn't recognize. They're imprinted with "Kindred Roots Café, Minneapolis."

"These cups are from a nice little place Ellen enjoys, not far from her home. I brought one back for each of us seeing as how we have Grass Roots in common. So, take yours home with you when you're done."

"Thanks, Murray. It's perfect! I'll use it in the microwave when I make tea."

Over dessert, Murray tells Delaney he taped the calendar for The Petri Dish to the front window of the shop, temporarily. He says he'll look into putting up a large bulletin board inside the store to post local musical events. Delaney tells him about meeting Kate and how appreciative she was that he carried Wolfe Creek's CD.

It's almost 9:30 p.m. when Delaney returns to her own place with her new coffee mug. She puts some music on and gets ready for bed, grateful for the recent turn of events in her life and her cozy little place. She picks up one of the new books and settles herself into the familiar depression of her futon.

Twenty-Four

Nick drains the rest of the coffee from his badly stained mug and punches buttons on his phone in a familiar sequence.

"Good Morning, Solano County District Attorney's Office. How may I direct your call?"

"Morning. Nick Barnes, Benicia PD. Is Karen Miller available?"

"Please hold, I'll put you through."

"This is Karen."

"Hi Karen. Nick Barnes. I'm calling about Liz Tanner, the victim in that domestic violence report I sent over yesterday."

"Yes." Karen pulls the file from a stack on her desk and reviews her notes. "I've left her a couple of messages, but she hasn't returned my calls."

"She's in the hospital. Took a face plant at the bottom of her driveway that knocked her out. Tox report shows THC and Percocet. She's got a couple of facial fractures including a badly broken nose. Hasn't come to. They're taking her into surgery this morning."

"Thanks for the update. I'm glad you managed to get some photos of her earlier injuries when you took her statement. Jeff is still in custody but without her cooperation, all I can hold him on right now is a violation of probation. His case is set for Friday morning. BAC was point one nine, so that'll stick. Given his DUI history, I'm going to ask the judge to impose a one-year sentence but consider myself lucky if I can get ninety days. You know how that goes."

"I definitely do."

"Nick, when you took Liz's statement, did you get an impression as to whether or not she'd be willing to testify?"

"I doubt it. She's a mess. You should see her place. When I got the call, I went over to secure it and brought the hospital her ID. She's got a marijuana card in her purse that looks legit. I'd like to meet that doctor. Her bathroom medicine cabinet looks like a miniature pharmacy but none of the bottles have her name on them. The place is a pig sty. I checked her answering machine in the kitchen. The light was on, but it said she had no messages. Looks like she deleted yours before she walked out of the house."

"Great. Does she have any family?"

"I haven't found anybody yet. The hospital is checking also. I'll keep you posted."

"Thanks Nick. I appreciate it."

Karen looks at the bruised face in the two photos clipped to the police report. The report says Liz is 36, two years younger than Karen but she looks to be about twenty years older. Karen closes the folder and sighs. She has a file drawer full of these cases, about half of which couldn't be prosecuted because the victim wasn't willing to testify against her abuser. She hates to think about the twisted trap these women find themselves in. Often it reaches back over several generations. "I hope you don't have a daughter," she says as she returns the file to the stack and answers another call.

Twenty-Five

Early Wednesday morning, Murray checks his answering machine. Someone named Luella had left a message for Delaney. He has time to deliver the message before opening the store.

"Morning, Murray," she says, towel-drying her hair.

"Hey, you might have a green thumb after all," he says, nodding toward the wooden container. "Maybe we'll even have enough tomatoes for a salad pretty soon. A woman named Luella left a message on the machine. She wants you to call but she didn't leave a number."

"Thanks. Can I come over and use your phone in a few minutes?"

"Sure. I've got to go open. Help yourself to the phone in the kitchen. Coffee too, if you want. Just made a pot."

Luella answers the phone in a voice that makes Delaney wonder if she's out of breath. "Are you okay?" she asks.

"I'm fine, sweetie. Just climbed a mountain of stairs with a basketful of laundry. We all share the facilities here and they're on the ground floor." She pauses for a moment. "I'm up on the third, which brings me to the reason why I called. First, though, tell me how Melody is doing so I can catch my breath and make some sense."

"Oh, she's doing a lot better. She's not limping as much as she was, and we've let her go back outside. Lyric seems curious about her bandage though. Murray was fine about the vet bill and glad I found the right doctor. He's already back to work in the shop so I have a day off."

"Well, I called because I had such a good time visiting with you the other day. I was wondering if you'd like to come over to my place and I could fix us a simple little dinner. It will have to be simple because I'm no fancy cook."

"Luella, that's so sweet of you. I'd love to," Delaney says, smiling to herself.

"How about tomorrow night then?"

"Tomorrow is fine, I'm not busy."

"I'll come over and get you at about four, so we can be ahead of the commuters on the freeway. At the risk of sounding nosy and impolite, I guess I should ask you if you're old enough for a glass of wine with dinner."

"Not technically. I'm seventeen."

"Well. A very mature seventeen, then. I'll see you tomorrow. I'm looking forward to it."

"Me too. Bye Luella."

Delaney lets herself out. After checking her email only to find spam, she shoulders her purse, locks the door and heads to Betty's to see if there's anything new.

A denim jacket catches her eye as soon as she walks in. It has some embroidered trim around the lapels and cuffs. Caught in the brightly colored threads are a few tiny seed and tube beads that reflect the light. Delaney takes it off the rack to get a closer look. It has another row of the same trim detail in the back. She tries it on and catches Betty smiling at her in the reflection from the mirror. The price is only $12.50 and it's in good shape. She can't imagine what it might have cost new. Delaney removes the jacket and hands it to Betty who puts it aside.

"Haven't seen you in a little while," Betty says.

"Been working. Glad I came by today though. I really like that jacket," Delaney says as she continues to browse.

In the book section, she finds an old cloth-bound hardback that she hasn't seen before. It's slim with no title on the spine. The title on the front cover faintly reads *History of The Donner Party: A Tragedy of the Sierra* (Fourteenth Edition) by C. F. McGlashan (Truckee, Calif.). She opens it to find it was copywritten in 1879 and 1880 and published in 1927. All the pages are intact, just a little yellowed around the edges. Betty has a $1.00 price sticker on it and Delaney feels sure it must be worth more than that. She remembers reading about the Donner Party in fourth grade and for that price, decides she's willing to do some research on the book and the author.

Instead of sitting down at her computer when she gets home, Delaney opens the book and begins to read. The more she reads, the more she realizes how much the harsh realities of this family's ordeal had been softened for retelling in a textbook written for nine-year-old children.

Delaney doesn't stop reading until she finishes the book late in the afternoon. She fixes herself a sandwich and then on an impulse, decides to get a haircut. At the very least, she knows she wants to get her bangs trimmed and some of the split ends cut off.

At the walk-in salon around the corner, Delaney flips through some hairstyle magazines while waiting her turn. The stylist is an older woman, maybe fifty or so, a little on the heavy side with bleached-blond hair twisted into a large tortoise shell clip at the back of her head. When she's called to the chair, Delaney tells her that she thinks she just wants a trim. After fastening the drape, the stylist gathers Delaney's hair in both hands, lifts it and pulls it away from her face.

"Do you see what I see?" she asks.

Delaney looks at herself in the mirror. "I don't know. What do you mean?"

"An absolutely beautiful face hidden behind a mask of makeup."

Delaney drops her gaze. She isn't sure how to respond and considers yanking the drape off and walking out.

The woman lets go of the hair and lightly rests her hands on Delaney's shoulders.

"I'm sorry, hon. In this line of work, I see a lot of faces and some of them definitely need help from a jar and a set of paints. Not yours. You have a natural beauty that is rare. Look at your eyes and your skin for crying out loud. If I'd had a face like yours, I could have been a model. Instead, I'm stuck behind a chair with a pair of scissors and a comb. Okay, so tell me what you want, and I'll shut up and start clipping."

In a way, Delaney begins to feel a little sorry for the woman. She takes a deep breath and tries to relax. "Maybe you could start with the bangs? I think they need to be a bit shorter."

"Would you mind if I feathered them, so we don't have such a straight edge?"

"I guess not," Delaney says. "Whatever you think."

"Okay, we'll see how that looks. Since you're the last customer of the day, we've got a little play time."

Almost an hour later, Delaney walks out of the shop feeling like a new person. Her hair is about six inches shorter and now falls in soft layers, just past her shoulders. She's anxious to get home and have another look. She also wants to wash her face. Maybe it was the lighting in the salon or the way she looked when the stylist pulled back her hair, but she's suddenly self-conscious about her makeup.

Delaney is walking up the driveway, when she sees Murray, carrying a bag of trash to the dumpster in the back.

"Looking for Delaney?" he asks with a smile. "She left here a little while ago."

She grins and feels color rise to her face.

"Hey. You look nice."

"Well, different, I guess. Thanks," she says, putting her key in the lock.

Twenty-Six

Luella cuts a couple of smoked sausages lengthwise, slices them into half-rounds, adds them to her skillet and adjusts the heat. Next, she rinses lentils and sets them aside. She wants to have everything ready ahead of time to put her lentil soup together. A bowl of diced carrots and onion is already sitting in the refrigerator. She wipes her hands on her apron and stirs the sausage, glancing at the clock on the kitchen wall. It's almost time to leave. Another minute or two on the sausage then she'll drain the grease off and put everything in the fridge until she gets back.

How could a girl have absolutely nobody? That question eats at Luella, but she doesn't want to probe too deeply. She reminds herself to be careful and go easy.

Luella arrives at Delaney's promptly at 4 o'clock and knocks. When Delaney opens the door, Luella can't believe her eyes. It's not just the new hairstyle. The thickly applied makeup is gone. Delaney's beautiful blue eyes shine brightly and her skin glows. She wears only a hint of smoky colored eyeshadow, mascara and lip gloss. Luella is amazed at the transformation.

"Well, I'll be," she says. "What a truly beautiful girl you are."

They give each other a warm hug. "It was kind of a spur of the moment thing. I had to do it quick before I changed my mind. I thought I'd just get a trim, but the lady was really nice and spent some extra time with my hair."

"Are you happy with the new style?" Luella asks.

"Well, I wasn't sure at first because it's so different, but I like it. My whole head feels lighter since my hair isn't as long. Murray said he likes it too."

Delaney locks the door and retrieves the cat carrier from Murray's back steps.

"I cleaned this out. I don't think we'll need it anymore for Melody. The bandage is off now, and her leg is healing just perfectly." Delaney puts it into Luella's trunk.

On the drive to Oakland, they both have their windows rolled down in the Taurus. The afternoon sun is still plenty warm and it's good to feel a breeze coming in off the bay. Luella pulls into her assigned parking spot under the building and accepts Delaney's offer to take the carrier upstairs. Luella leads the way, three flights up the open concrete staircase, pausing briefly at each landing before going on. From the stairs, a common courtyard with a swimming pool surrounded by a fence is visible.

"It must be nice to have a pool on days like this," Delaney says.

"I suppose," Luella replies, a little out of breath as she searches for her keys in her purse. "My problem is I never learned how to swim. Once or twice when the temperature gets up into the triple digits, I've put my suit on and dipped myself in the shallow end just to cool off and boy does that feel good. Welcome to my humble abode," she says, pushing the door open and motioning for Delaney to step inside.

"Ooh, something smells good!" Delaney says.

"I was cooking some sausage before I left. You can set your bag anywhere you like. The carrier goes in that front closet over there. And here comes my roommate, Maisey."

Delaney crouches down and offers her hand to Luella's cat who pushes her head against it, wanting to be scratched. Delaney obliges and after a couple of minutes, she stands back up and looks around.

"This is a cool place, Luella. Is that your husband?" she asks, pointing to the bookshelf.

"That's my Harold. We were married twenty-eight years when he passed." Luella takes her apron off the hook and walks over and stands next to Delaney. "He was the kind of man so many women hope to find in their lifetime — not just a husband, but a true friend and partner in life. I'm so grateful for all the good times we had together before he became ill." Luella puts her apron on and places a large soup pot on the stove.

"Can I help you with anything?"

"Not really. I got most of this ready earlier so I'm just going to throw it together and turn it on. Why don't you pull up a stool there at the counter, so we can visit while I mix some cornbread to put in the oven?"

Delaney settles herself on the stool and watches Luella move about the kitchen.

"I hope one day I'll have kitchen as nice as this."

"Well, this one is pretty small as kitchens go, but it's well organized and I've always loved having a window over my kitchen sink, so I can look out while I'm doing dishes."

"I guess if I'm going to make good use of a kitchen someday, I should learn how to cook. My mother was only good at opening cans and heating things up. Kind of like what I do now."

"Can't do much more than that when all you have is a microwave and a cooler," Luella says. "You can still eat healthy though if you be sure to include plenty of fresh vegetables and fruit." Luella opens a cookbook to a well-used, spattered page and places it in a stand on her counter. "My mother preferred to make cornbread from a packaged mix, but I like to make it from scratch. Seems to taste better and really doesn't take that much longer. I'm going to have to ask you to cover your eyes though when I add my secret ingredient."

Delaney laughs. "It's something that's not in your cookbook recipe?"

"Well, it wouldn't be secret if it was, would it?" Luella smiles as she greases a heavy cast iron skillet and sets it on top of the stove. She stirs the wet and dry ingredients together in the mixing bowl and then says "Okay, it's time."

Delaney covers her eyes with both hands, resting her elbows on the counter. She hears Luella open and close the refrigerator door.

"No peeking." Luella glances at Delaney. *This poor child never saw her momma cook.* "Oh, all right. I'll share my secret. I guess your cooking lessons might as well start right here."

Delaney uncovers her eyes and Luella holds up a small container of sour cream. She hands Delaney a soup spoon from the drawer and tells her to scoop out a big heaping spoonful.

"I don't need to measure it?"

"Nope. My secret is just one big spoonful. Perfect. Now drop it right in here." Luella pushes the mixing bowl toward her on the counter. Delaney watches the sour cream fall into the bowl and then asks if she can lick the spoon. "That's part of the cooking," Luella says as she mixes in the sour cream and then pours the batter into the skillet. "Sour cream keeps the cornbread from crumbling and makes it moist. Now you guard that secret until you have a little girl of your own one day." Luella slides the skillet into the oven.

Delaney goes into the kitchen to lift the lid on the soup. "That smells so good I can hardly wait."

"Let's set the table and then I'll give you the ten-cent tour of my place," Luella says.

Returning to the living room, Luella reaches for a small spiral address book she keeps on her desk. "I'd like to add you to my little book, and it occurs to me that I don't even know your last name."

Delaney hesitates for a moment before responding. "Moran, M-O-R-A-N."

Luella flips the "D" tab and carefully writes it down. "I always file by first name because that's how I remember people. Drove Harold crazy. Do you use the address of the music store for your mail?"

"No. I rent a mailbox at The Office. My place doesn't have an address of its own since it's still supposed to be a garage."

"So, if I wanted to send you a card or something, then where would I send it?" Luella asks, her pen poised over the little book.

Delaney gives her the address and the box number. "I thought it was kind of lucky I got that box number because it's the month and day that I was born so it's easy to remember."

Luella jots the address down, then looks at Delaney. "February? If I was to believe in astrology, I would have guessed that you were born in September, a Virgo, because your little place is so well organized."

Delaney shrugs. "No, Aquarius. I don't pay much attention to that anyway." She pulls a scrap of paper out of her purse. "Okay, now I need your info, so I can add it to my contacts on the computer. First, do you have an email address?"

"Honey, I don't even have a computer. I used one at the office when I was still working, you know, just to get on our agency's database, but I've never had my own. I don't know how to do all that Internet surfing stuff anyway. It's all I can do to put a CD or video in those machines over there and get them to play. I don't even have a cell phone."

The timer buzzes. Luella takes the cornbread out of the oven and sets it on top of the stove. She gives the soup a stir and turns the burner off. "Time to eat."

Delaney is looking at Luella, waiting.

"Oh, right. My address," Luella says.

Delaney writes it down. "What about your birthday?" Delaney asks.

"May fourth will do it. For the year, we'll just say I'm over thirty. Nobody's gonna argue with that. There's a pitcher of iced tea in the refrigerator, Delaney, and you'll see a little bowl of honey butter. Please get those." Luella puts a hot pad on the table and brings the cornbread over. "Let's just serve our soup from the stove." She hands Delaney her bowl. "Beauty before age. You go first."

"Have you always lived in Vallejo?" Luella asks, after they sit down.

"Yes, since I was born." Delaney lifts her plate and Luella serves her a wedge of steaming hot cornbread. "What about you?"

"I was born in Sacramento and my family moved down here just before I started school. My father got hired on to work for the Key System Rail Line here in the East Bay. After that shut down, he went to work for AC Transit. My mother stayed at home and raised my little brother and I."

"Where's your brother now?"

"Raymond teaches school in San Jose. He has a lovely wife and two very smart boys. One is going off to college in a month or so and the other is still in high school." Luella showed Delaney a framed picture of her brother and his family. "I'm very proud of my nephews. The oldest one there, he's always on me to get a computer. Says after he goes to school we can stay in touch on the 'My Place' or some such. I tell him I can stay in touch just fine with my telephone."

"Luella, this dinner is so good. It's the best I've had in a long time."

"Well, I made plenty and there's only one of me, so I'll fix you some to take home later."

After dinner, Luella walks Delaney down to the community room and shows her the shelves of movies. She explains that some residents donate movies they no longer want, and these are available for borrowing anytime. Delaney chooses *Thelma and Louise* and they go back upstairs. Luella makes popcorn and they settle on the loveseat with Maisey curled up at Delaney's feet.

It's almost 10 o'clock when Luella takes Delaney back home. Pulling in behind the VW, she sees a curtain move in Murray's window that overlooks the driveway. Delaney gets out with two containers of leftovers. She sets them on the hood of the car as Luella comes around the front to give her a hug.

"I had so much fun tonight Luella. Thank you for everything."

"It was absolutely my pleasure and I hope we'll be together again real soon. You are a blessing to me Delaney."

Luella waits until Delaney is safely inside before getting back in her car and driving away.

Twenty-Seven

Liz's eyes are closed. Her face is wrapped in bandages. The room is quiet except for the ticking of the clock on the wall and an occasional soft beep from the IV monitor.

"Miss Tanner? Miss Tanner, can you hear me?" A nurse touches Liz's arm lightly. No response. She takes Liz's vital signs and makes notations on her chart. There have been no visitors and no flowers or cards have arrived since Liz was brought down from the recovery room earlier today. Both beds were unoccupied when she arrived, and the orderlies put her in the bed nearest the window. The nurse opens the blinds all the way, letting the afternoon sun fall across the foot of Liz's bed. She checks urine output from the catheter and inspects the IV bag. When she pulls the curtain between beds to give Liz a little more privacy, the ball bearings jangle in their metal track above and the nurse notices Liz's eyelids flutter ever so slightly. She moves in closer to Liz and speaks her name softly. Liz opens her eyes with what appears to be great effort and seems to have trouble focusing.

"Hello Miss Tanner." Liz's eyes wander around the room. The nurse speaks slowly and carefully.

"You are in the hospital because you had a fall. We need you to rest."

Liz raises her right hand just a little, but the effort seems to be too much. Her eyes close and she surrenders to sleep. The nurse checks her watch, charts the response and steps out to call the doctor.

When Officer Barnes is notified Liz has come through the surgery and is beginning to come around, he contacts Karen Miller. Karen assures him she'll call the nurse's station in the morning to see if a visit will be possible.

Later that afternoon, Nick drops by the hospital and finds Liz's doctor at her bedside. He waits in the doorway. The doctor glances toward the door and sees the uniform. He discreetly holds up his hand, indicating Nick should not enter the room. Nick leans against the wall outside the door and listens carefully. He does not hear Liz speak.

Several minutes later, the doctor steps out and motions for Nick to follow him down the hall to a small conference room. They exchange introductions.

"Considering the impact, I think she's pretty lucky. In addition to the broken nose, the CT scan revealed a complex malar fracture of the right cheekbone. We did an open reduction to position the three broken pieces of the bone and they've been stabilized with small metal screws and a plate. Unfortunately, this means she'll have an obvious scar across that cheek. Both orbital bones were remarkably intact, so her vision should be unaffected. If all goes well, she'll be here for three more days. She should have someone at home for the first couple of weeks when she's released."

"Does she understand where she is and what happened?" Nick asks.

"I've briefly explained the injuries to her, but I don't know that she's able to take it all in just yet. We've begun administering pain medication through her IV. Right now, we need her to rest. I'll come by during my morning rounds and we'll see if she's better able to respond by voice. Would you mind waiting until tomorrow to visit?"

"Sure."

"It might be best if you're not in uniform. I'd like to avoid causing any anxiety for her. When you talk to her, if she seems at all distressed, I'll ask you to cut your visit short."

"I understand, doctor." Nick extended his hand. "Thank you for all you've done. One question — if she doesn't have anyone at home to help her, are there other options?"

"Only on a very short-term basis. I might be able to arrange for a bed at a care facility for a week or so, then she'd be on her own. See what you can do."

Back at the police station, Nick reviews his notes again. Although he didn't write it down, he distinctly remembers Liz telling him she has a daughter that was coming over to stay with her the night Jeff was arrested.

Twenty-Eight

L uella wakes up early, eager to shower, dress and drive over to the Solano County government offices. She purposely chooses her sage green summer suit and straw hat. Pertinent information is written on an index card she tucks into her purse and she checks to be sure she still has a few of her old business cards in her wallet, just in case.

In the Office of Vital Records, Luella asks to search the index of birth records from seventeen years ago. The young black woman who assists her is friendly and helpful, but the number of records is daunting. How many births could there be in one county in one month? Luella scrolls through the records, reminding herself that God rewards patience.

About twenty minutes into the task, she finds a birth record for Delaney Renee Moran, born February first in Vallejo. It lists her mother as Elizabeth Ann Tanner, age 17 and her father as Marty Moran, no middle name, age 18. California is listed as the birth state for both parents. Luella notes all this information on the back of her index card and returns it to her purse. She recalls there being certain limitations imposed as to who can obtain an official copy of a birth certificate, but she doesn't need a copy — only the information. She finds the clerk who assisted her and asks if it would be possible to research earlier birth records, thinking perhaps one or both of Delaney's parents might have also been born in Solano County.

"Do you know what month you're looking for?" the young woman asks.

"No, I don't. I've got plenty of time on my hands this morning though and this is kind of important to me, so if you don't mind, I'll just make myself comfortable. If somebody else needs the machine, let me know and I'll scoot."

Luella settles herself back into the seat and checks the clock. With a bit of quick math and some luck, she could be out of here by noon. Scanning the birth records by month, she looks for both names at the same time. She figures it's a bit of a long shot but easier than writing to Sacramento and having to wait several weeks for a reply. It doesn't take too long before she begins to wonder how people can sit in front of a screen for eight hours a day without going blind. Over an hour into her search, a birth record for an Elizabeth Ann Tanner turns up with the date of October 13th. Luella pulls out her pen and writes down the names of the man and woman she hopes are Delaney's grandparents: Keith Wade and Doris Leanne (Cooper) Tanner. At the time of Elizabeth's birth, Keith was 20 and Doris, 18.

Noticing her leg beginning to cramp, Luella decides to forego further research on Marty for the moment. If she hits a dead end with Elizabeth Ann, she'll come back and pick up where she left off. Luella thanks the clerk for her help as she leaves the office.

On the way home, Luella picks up a copy of the *Times-Herald*. Back at her apartment, she draws a crude-looking family tree on a piece of paper. This was something she used to do when she was working a case, particularly for families with tangled branches. With a pencil, she fills in the information she has so far, and considers what steps to take next.

First, she checks her wallet to see if she still has her library card. She pulls all sorts of discount coupons, punch cards, business cards and folded receipts out of the overstuffed sections and finally locates it. Calling the phone number on the back, she reserves a computer workstation at the local branch for the following morning. That done, she fixes a sandwich, telling herself her mind will work better on a full stomach.

Luella scans the obituaries in the paper while she eats. She scratches some figures in the margin to calculate the approximate ages of Delaney's grandparents. If Keith and Doris are the right folks, they would most likely still be alive. She decides she'll check death records though, just in case, again reminding herself she's making some pretty big assumptions.

Luella takes another index card and begins making a "to do" list on one side. On the other side, she jots down other types of public records she could check such as newspapers, property records, court cases. She hopes she'll find a kind person at the library, willing to show her how to do a search by name on the Internet.

Twenty-Nine

Murray is on the phone when a young man walks into the store. He doesn't seem to be looking for anything in particular — just sort of standing around with his hands stuffed into the pockets of some fairly tight jeans.

"Hi there. Can I help you find something?" Murray asks after he hangs up.

"Uh, I was looking for Delaney. Is she working today?" the young man asks, looking past Murray to the rear of the store.

"No, not today I'm afraid," Murray answers cautiously. "I'd be happy to take a message for her though."

"Uh. Okay. Could you ask her to give me a call?" He removes his hands from his pockets and pats himself as though looking for something to write with.

Murray puts a piece of scratch paper and a pen on the counter. "Why don't you write down your name and number and I'll see she gets it."

The young man extends his hand and says, "I'm Julian. A friend of hers."

They shake hands. Julian writes his number down on the paper, gives it to Murray, thanks him and leaves. Murray waits several minutes before taking the note next door. His knock goes unanswered. Deciding he doesn't want to tuck it into the door jamb, he brings the note back to the store.

Later that evening, when Delaney comes over to wash a load of laundry, Murray remembers the note.

"A young man named Julian came into the shop looking for you about eleven o'clock this morning. Left his number and asked you to give him a call." Murray hands her the note.

"Oh, okay. Thanks Murray."

"He said he was a friend of yours. I wasn't sure if you told him where you live, so I didn't send him next door. You'll have to pardon my erring on the side of caution."

"No problem, Murray. That's okay. I get it. Can I use your phone?"

"Help yourself, hon."

Delaney slips into the kitchen and Murray retreats to his bedroom to give her a little privacy. A few minutes later, she hangs up the phone. Murray comes out of his room with a dirty coffee cup and rinses it in the sink.

"He's an okay guy, Murray. He's the one I told you about that works as part of the stage crew for The Petri Dish. I'm gonna go down to the Bean and meet him for a cup of coffee. Do you need me to bring you anything while I'm out?" Delaney asks.

"No, I think I'm set. Thanks, though. Have a good time."

Back at her place, Delaney changes into a soft, pale blue ribbed sweater. As she combs her hair, it occurs to her that Julian hasn't seen her since she'd gotten it cut. She puts on a little makeup, some lip gloss and a pair of silver earrings that dangle a crescent moon from one ear and a star from the other. She brings the new denim jacket with her.

Julian is waiting for her outside the Bean when she arrives. He's looking down the street and doesn't recognize her until she's just a few yards away.

"Delaney? Wow, you look great!" He gives her a quick hug then walks around her in a circle. "Nice hair. I really like it. You look totally hot, if you don't mind my saying so."

"I don't mind," she says, smiling, as he opens the door for her.

Julian pays for their coffee drinks and a slice of Death by Chocolate cake and leads her over to a corner table.

"Hey. Thanks for coming to meet me. It's good to see you again. I wanted a chance to apologize for being a bit of a jerk the last time we saw each other. I shouldn't have left you here waiting while I had a beer with the band. I'm sorry." He pushes the plate toward her.

"It's sweet of you to apologize but I just sort of figured it was a good move for you, business-wise, especially since you seem to be branching out into PR. Anyway, no worries Julian." She takes tiny a bite of cake and rolls her eyes. "Oh, my God, this is the best cake I've ever had." Delaney picks up another piece with the fork and starts to offer it to Julian when he leans forward and opens his mouth.

He savors his bite for a moment with his eyes closed then licks his lips. "If this cake is gonna kill us, then it's not a bad way to go." He takes the fork from her hand and feeds another bite to her. They take turns, cutting each bite smaller to make it last, until every bit of the dark chocolate frosting has been scraped clean from the plate.

Over coffee and refills, Julian tells Delaney about his work. She tells him about her new friend, Luella, and about how much she enjoyed working in Murray's shop. She asks Julian where he lives, and he explains, sort of sheepishly, that he still lives at home with his folks.

"I've given myself a goal of moving out by the first of the year. My father doesn't have any confidence in me being able to save money on my own, so they've been taking half the rent I've been paying and putting it into a savings account, so I'll have a deposit for a place. It makes me feel like I'm being micro-managed, but I try not to get too worked up about it. Other than that, we stay out of each other's way. What about your folks? Do you see them much?" he asks.

"No. I've never had any contact with my father and my mother is a total loser." Delaney picks up a napkin and squeezes it into a tight little ball. "I moved out of her place a little over a year ago. Too much drama. It's like she's a professional victim or something, with one abusive boyfriend after another. It's pretty sick."

"Damn. I'm sorry Delaney. Good thing you're able to make it on your own."

"It's not easy, but basically, I just couldn't stand to hang around and look at her bruises anymore. She wore them like medals, like she'd earned them. When the guy of the week wasn't around to beat her up, she'd sit in front of the computer, smoking weed and listening to oldies. It's pathetic."

"Weed? Really?"

"She talked some doctor into giving her one of those medical permits. Claimed she had arthritis or something. Anyway, forget about her."

"Okay, so do you have any other family around here?" he asks.

"Nope. That's it."

"No grandparents?"

"No, Julian. All I've ever had was her. She told me her parents were dead and my dad took off." Delaney shifts in her seat. "Can we talk about something else?"

"Yeah. Sure. Have you ever been to the Japanese Tea Garden in San Francisco?"

"No. Where did that come from?"

"The tea garden? Probably Japan."

She grins. "No. The question."

"I don't know. It was the first thing that popped into my mind when you said you wanted to change the subject. Anyway, would you like to go? We could take the ferry over and catch a bus."

"Um, yeah, I guess," she says.

"Good. I'm off day after tomorrow and it's less busy during the week so it's a good time to go. Whaddya think?"

"I think I can fit it into my schedule," she says with a smile.

"Can I walk you home again tonight?"

"I was hoping you would."

When they leave the Bean, Julian takes Delaney's hand in his as they walk up the street.

Thirty

Nick Barnes steps out of the elevator at the hospital the next morning, wearing a colorful Hawaiian shirt over his navy-blue uniform pants. He carries a vase of cheery chrysanthemums and stops at the nurse's station briefly, to show his badge.

"Good morning Officer Barnes. Our patient, Ms. Tanner, didn't sleep well last night, and she was very restless this morning. Her doctor came by a little while ago and gave her something to help her relax. If she has fallen asleep, could you postpone your visit until this afternoon?" the nurse asks.

"Of course. I'll just quietly poke my head in to see how she's doing."

Nick walks over and stands in the doorway of Liz's room. The first bed is still unoccupied, so he takes a few steps in and peers around the curtain. Liz's eyes are open. He goes around to the window side of her bed.

"Good morning, Liz. I'll just set these over here," he says, putting the vase on the windowsill. When he stands next to the rail of her bed, she turns her head ever so slightly in his direction.

"Are you able to talk, Liz?"

"Yes," she says, her voice barely above a whisper.

"Do you remember who I am?"

"No." She looks at his dark brown, neatly trimmed hair and tries to remember if she ever knew anyone who looked like that. She tries not to look at his shirt. The colors and pattern bother her eyes.

"I'm one of the officers who helped you the other night. I understand you took a bad fall on your driveway."

Liz doesn't respond.

"I fixed the lock on your front door for you, so you don't need to worry about your house."

"Thank you." She points to the cup of water with a straw in it on her tray table.

Nick picks it up. Bending toward her, he gently guides the straw into her mouth. Liz takes a sip, then motions with her hand for him to put it back.

"Liz, your doctor wants to keep you here for a couple more days and then he'd like you to have someone at home with you to help you for a little while. I remember you told me you have a daughter. I'd like to contact her for you."

"No," Liz says, very clearly.

Nick notices her breathing pattern is becoming more rapid. "You don't want her to come and stay with you?" he asks.

"No."

"Is there someone else I could contact for you?"

"Jeff."

"Liz, Jeff won't be available for a while. The judge has ordered him to remain in custody at least for now." Nick can tell by the look in her eyes that she is becoming slightly agitated. "We don't have to settle this today," he says. "The most important thing for you to do is to rest and let your body heal. I'm going to leave so you can do that. Would you like another sip of water before I go?"

"No."

Nick reaches for her hand and Liz pulls it away, stiffening. He waves good-bye and after leaving the room, stops by the nurse's station on his way to the elevator.

"She was awake, but I think she wants to rest now, so I'm going to leave. Here's my card in case she asks for me. I doubt she will, but you never know. Good day ladies."

At the patrol car, Nick changes back into his uniform shirt and puts on the rest of his gear.

Before heading to the station, he drives over to Liz's house to see if either of her neighbors are home. Pulling into the court, he notices a car in the driveway of the home immediately to the left of Liz's house. Nick parks his vehicle and goes up to the door. An elderly woman in a housedress answers his knock.

"Good morning, ma'am. I'm sorry for disturbing you. May we speak for a moment?"

"Yes, of course, officer. Please come in," she says, opening the door. She gestures toward her living room and offers him a seat.

Nick notices the mustard colored shag carpet and outdated furnishings and feels for a moment that he's entered a time warp. He detects a slight mothball fragrance, that for a moment, reminds him of his grandmother's home. Almost every flat surface has a figurine perched on a doily. A television in the corner looks like it's out of the '50s. Nick sits in a stiff-backed chair, fingering his hat.

"Would you like something to drink?"

"No, thank you. This won't take long. I'd just like to ask you a couple of questions if I may."

She perches on the edge of the couch, her hands folded in her lap.

"Do you know your neighbor Ms. Tanner very well?"

"Yes, I'd have to say unfortunately, I do. I understand she fell at the bottom of her driveway the other day. Drugs and alcohol, no doubt."

"She's in the hospital recovering from her injuries and I'm trying to locate her daughter," he said.

"Oh, Delaney? Well, good luck. She used to live with her mother, but I haven't seen her in a year or so, not since she flew the coop. I don't blame her one bit, either. Wherever she is, I'm sure she's better off."

Nick made a note on a small pad he pulled from his pocket. "Is her last name Tanner also, do you know?"

"No, I don't think so. I'm pretty sure she had a different last name. I can't recall it though."

"Do you have any idea where Delaney might be living?"

"No, I'm sorry I don't."

"Well, thank you for your time, ma'am. I appreciate it."

Nick hands her his card.

"You're very welcome, officer. I'm sorry I wasn't able to be of more help."

In the car, Nick radios dispatch to advise he is en route to the local high school.

~

The secretary in the main office directs Nick to the counseling department down the hall. At the door, Nick waits while two students finish their business at the reception desk. They are slow to leave, apparently curious about his visit.

"Back to class boys," the secretary seems friendly but firm. They shuffle out the door.

"Good afternoon, officer. What can I do for you?"

"I'm looking for information about a former student, first name of Delaney. I don't have her last name."

"That sounds familiar. We're able to do a first name search in our system but it will take a minute or two for me to log into archived records."

"No problem."

"Here we go. Her last name is M-O-R-A-N and it looks like she missed her diploma by just a few credits. Do you need a printout of the student info screen?"

"I'd appreciate it."

The secretary pulls the page off the printer and hands it to him. "She's a pretty girl. I hope everything is alright."

"Thank you for your help." Nick tips his hat.

As he had expected, the home address on the record was the address of Liz's house. At least now he has a grainy photo image and a last name. Nick calls Karen Miller to share this information. He also tells her about his visit with Liz in the hospital.

"She tensed up noticeably when I told her Jeff would be in custody for a while. The night Jeff was arrested, she told me her daughter was coming over to stay with her and now it seems pretty clear she doesn't want her daughter around."

"Could be they've had a falling out since then," Karen surmises. "If I came home and found my mother in that kind of shape, you can bet we'd have a falling out, too."

"I don't know. I'm going to do a little more digging this afternoon. If I find anything, I'll let you know. They gave Liz some meds this morning, so you might want to check with the nurses if you're planning a visit."

After working through phone and email messages, Nick checks police records for Delaney Moran. Nothing turns up. He fills his coffee cup and does an Internet search for her. Before his coffee even begins to cool, he finds an address for a Delaney Moran, in Vallejo.

Thirty-One

Luella arrives at the library fifteen minutes early, signs in at the reference desk and presents her library card. The officious-looking librarian delivers her refrain.

"Workstation sessions are limited to one hour. A reminder message will appear when five minutes remain. At sixty minutes, your session will be terminated."

Luella notices a young man sorting books on a cart behind the librarian. He looks a little too young to be an employee. She raises her voice just a little.

"Would you happen to have someone who could show me how to do a search on the Internet? I know how to point and click but I'm afraid that's about it."

The librarian, clearly annoyed, sighs.

"Devon," she says, turning to the young man, "would you please help this patron for a moment on workstation number seven?"

"Sure," he says coming around the counter.

As they walk over to the row of computers, Luella asks if he works there.

"No, ma'am. I'm a student volunteer. I have to do community service hours to graduate and they let some of us do them here."

Devon pulls a chair up next to Luella and shows her how to bring up the Internet browser.

"I'm very grateful for your help. I need to research death records and I also want to do a general search for someone by name."

"Just type the name you want to look up in that little box," he says, indicating with his finger.

Wanting to protect Delaney's privacy while Devon looks over her shoulder, Luella types in the name of her best friend from high school.

"Now click on that search button."

Almost immediately, a list of results appears. Devon tells her she can click on any one of them to read more.

"Watch for a tiny hand to appear before you click. You can use this back arrow up here to go back to your previous page."

"You young folks have taken to this technology like fish to water. It's all I can do to try to find the right button on my TV remote," Luella says.

"You'll get the hang of it pretty quick," Devon assures her. "To find a place to look up death records, just type 'death records' in the search bar like you did with the name. If you need to have something printed, I can help you with that. I'll be here for another hour."

Luella thanks Devon for his help and he tells her to ask for him again at the reference desk if she gets stuck. Under the watchful eye of the librarian, he returns to his cart.

Luella carefully follows his instructions and several clicks later finds her way to a site that lets her check the Social

Security Death Index for free. Eager to begin, she types in Doris Tanner, the person she believes to be Delaney's grandmother. To narrow her search, she selects California as the state of residence at time of death.

Waiting for results, she watches the little green bar at the bottom of the screen, expecting there to be no record, since Doris would likely be close to her own age by now. A moment later, a match appears. Luella reads that Doris Leanne Tanner died in Vallejo at the age of 39, one month before Delaney was born. No cause of death was listed.

Stunned, Luella sits back in her seat and stares at the screen in disbelief. She takes a deep breath and reaches for a scrap of paper and a stubby pencil from the box next to the computer. Her hand is shaking as she jots down this information. Next, she clicks the back arrow a couple of times and enters Keith's name. This search ends with the message "match not found" leading her to believe Delaney's grandfather is still alive. Luella glances at the clock on the computer. Twenty minutes remain in her session.

Returning to the home page, she does a general search for Liz Tanner and Keith Tanner that results in a confusing array of genealogical sites. She can't find anything useful before the five-minute warning appears. Luella returns to the login screen, puts her notes in her purse and stops by the reference desk to thank Devon again before leaving.

In the familiar cocoon of her car, Luella puts her key in the ignition and bangs her hand on the steering wheel in frustration. Her eyes well up and she reaches into the glove box for a tissue. She can't decide who she feels worse for — Delaney never having known her grandmother or her grandmother never having known Delaney. It is such a huge loss for them both.

Luella flips her visor down and checks herself in the mirror. She shakes her head and applies some lipstick. When she feels she has regained her composure, she drives back to the Office of Vital Records in Solano County. The same young clerk who had helped her before, greets her at the counter. Luella explains that this time she needs to research a death certificate.

"This will be a good deal easier, since you have the name and date of death," the clerk says, walking Luella over to the terminal. She pulls up the death record search screen.

"If you find the record and want a copy, let me know. I can give you what we call an 'informational use only' copy for a small charge."

"Thank you, dear," Luella says. She enters Doris Tanner's name and waits. In a matter of seconds, an image of the death certificate appears on the screen. Luella scrolls down to find the cause of death which reads, "asphyxiation, due to, or as a consequence of, smoke inhalation resulting from a structure fire."

"Oh, my dear Lord," Luella exclaims out loud. "That poor, poor woman." Luella pulls a wad of tissue from her pocket and blows her nose. As she gets up to leave, her body seems to feel heavier than it did when she sat down. Moving slowing toward her car, she realizes there is still so much she doesn't know and yet she feels almost overwhelmed by what she's learned in the past couple of days.

Distracted by her thoughts, she doesn't see the newspaper rack on the sidewalk and bumps right into it. "Ouch!" Rubbing her hip, she notices the day's edition, pressed up against the glass. *The newspaper. Of course!* She drops three quarters into the machine, pulls out a copy and spreads it on the hood of her car, opening to the second page to find the address of the newspaper office.

Thirty-Two

In the locker room at the end of his day shift, Nick changes into civilian clothes — khaki slacks and a light blue, striped shirt. He sends his wife a text message:

Taking a detour thru Vallejo on the way home. Shouldn't be long.

Nick's suspicion that the box number in the address indicates a mailbox business is confirmed when he pulls up in front of The Office. He glances at the business hours on the door as he holds it open for a middle-aged woman who is walking out with a large package in her arms. There are no other customers inside when Nick enters and approaches the man behind the counter. He notices the name "Alex" on the badge pinned to his shirt.

"Good afternoon," he says. "I'm looking for someone by the name of Delaney Moran and I understand she may be one of your boxholders."

Alex's mouth works itself into a smirking grin. "Maybe. Maybe not. I guess it depends on who wants to know."

Nick pulls his badge out of his pocket and lays it on the counter. He sees Alex straighten up and he slips it back into his pocket.

"Benicia Police Department, huh? Aren't you a little out of your jurisdiction, officer?" Alex asks.

"Very observant of you. If you have a problem with that, Alex, I can have one of your local officers up here in a patrol car in a matter of minutes."

"What do you need to know? Is she in some kind of trouble?"

"I'll answer your first question. I need to know where she lives."

Alex opens a drawer in a file cabinet below the counter and rifles through some hanging files. He shoves a piece of paper across the counter.

"This is her rental agreement. She's had the box for about a year."

Nick notices the address given for her residence is a Vallejo address.

"Need me to make you a copy?" Alex asks.

"No, that's not necessary," Nick says, pulling out his notebook and writing down the address. No phone number was provided on the form. "How often would you say she comes in to check her mail?" he asks.

"Her mail? She almost never gets any mail here. Comes in a couple times a week I guess and occasionally ships packages. That's about it."

Nick nods. He tears a piece of paper out of his notebook and writes:

"Delaney — Please give me a call when you get this note. It's not an emergency and you're not in trouble. Thank you, Nick Barnes."

He grabs the stapler on the counter, staples one of his business cards to the note and folds it in half.

"Can I trouble you for an envelope?" he asks.

Alex puts a small white envelope on the counter. Nick tucks the note inside, seals it and writes "Delaney Moran, Box 201" on the front. He hands the envelope to Alex.

"I'd appreciate it if you'd put this in her box."

"Yes, sir," Alex says with a two-finger salute.

Nick thanks him and leaves. Locating the address Delaney provided on the form, he finds a vacant building in an old part of town that had last seen life ages ago as an appliance repair shop. Nick drives around the corner and turns into the alley that runs behind the buildings. He shuts off his engine, glances around and walks to the back of that building, immediately picking up the pungent stench of urine. There are iron bars over the windows, and someone has nailed a heavy sheet of plywood over the back door. A rat skitters behind a pile of trash next to the steps. A rusted shopping cart with an old blanket stuffed inside is shoved up against the building. Nick returns to his car and heads home, hoping to receive a call soon.

Thirty-Three

Delaney wakes up smiling, thinking about Julian and their time together the night before. She'd invited him in after he walked her home and they'd talked for another couple of hours over tea. He seemed surprised and impressed by the framed spider webs on her wall, admitting he was also fascinated by spiders and would sometimes spend several minutes watching them weave their webs or wind their magical threads around prey. Sitting closely together on the futon, he confessed to sometimes deliberately dropping a small live bug onto a spider's web and then waiting to watch the attack.

"When I was in fifth grade, I had a tarantula named Nancy. She'd let me hold her," Julian told her. "It drove my mother crazy."

"How did you know Nancy was a female?"

Julian reached over and traced Delaney's mouth with his finger.

"I could tell by her lips."

Delaney closes her eyes, feeling a warm tingle as she remembers the way he leaned over and gently kissed her in that moment. She'd lost herself in that kiss and wanted more. Before she could ask him to stay the night, he'd pulled himself away.

"I should go Delaney. I like you and I want to see you again."

Standing, he'd reached for her hand and pulled her to her feet.

Delaney recalls feeling a bit confused, both disappointed and relieved. They'd said good night at her door and gave each other a warm hug before he walked down the driveway, disappearing in the dark.

In her bathrobe, Delaney lingers over her coffee and checks her email, disappointed that nothing else has sold. She looks under her table and quickly takes a rough inventory. Realizing she hasn't labeled her Post-it notes with the date she put the item up for sale, she decides to go through her account online and do this to get a better idea of how long she's had some of the items. She still has room under the table and plans to visit Betty's and Repeats after she gets dressed, to see if anything new or interesting has turned up.

Wendy notices Delaney's hair as soon as she walks in.

"Hey, your hair looks great!" she says. "I've been trying to scare up the courage to do something different with mine, but I always chicken out. So here I am. Bad hair day, every day."

"Thanks," Delaney says, smiling. "I've decided I'm happy with it."

"You've done something different with your face, too. Damn, you've just done a whole makeover. You really look good."

"Thanks. Anything new come in lately?" Delaney asks, feeling a little self-conscious.

"A few things," Wendy says, as she comes around the counter. "Here, I'll show you."

Delaney follows her through the shop as she points out a couple of small digital cameras, a pair of ski boots, a large painting of a clipper ship, clothing and a couple of jewelry items. Delaney asks to see a pendant hanging on a gold chain and Wendy hands it to her. It was an odd match, as though the chain didn't originally come with the pendant. The pendant was oval — an enameled floral design in a setting with a gold-tone scalloped border. Delaney is pretty sure the pendant is a piece of costume jewelry, but she can't be sure about the chain. At $15 for both, it's a gamble. She looks at the cameras, priced at $20 each. Not knowing a lot about cameras, that seems a gamble, too. She decides to take the pendant and chain.

"I hope this is a gift," Wendy says. "I don't think it's really your style."

"You're right. It's not. Could be though if I hang onto it for about forty years."

They both laugh.

"Later Wendy."

After she rounds the corner, Delaney slips the pendant off the chain, drops it into her purse, then fastens the chain around her neck. Passing by a jewelry store, she steps inside. A middle-aged woman behind the counter looks up.

"What can I do for you young lady?"

"Do you think you'd be able to tell if my chain is made of real gold? It was a gift and I'm just curious."

"If you can take it off, I'd be happy to look at it for you," the woman says.

Delaney removes the chain and hands it to her. She takes it over to a bright table lamp and puts her glasses on. A moment later, she returns.

"If this is from a gentleman, then I would say he's a keeper," she says, handing the chain back to Delaney. "The design is what we call a 'wheat' pattern and this particular one is genuine fourteen karat gold in a lovely eighteen-inch length. Wear it in good health my dear. I have some earrings over here I could show you that would complement that chain nicely."

"I'll bring him in with me, so he can help me pick out a pair," Delaney says, trying not to appear giddy. "Thank you for looking at the chain for me."

"My pleasure, dear."

Delaney doesn't see Betty when she stops by her store a few minutes later. Another woman is at the register waiting on a customer. Delaney notices the bookshelf appears to have been restocked since she was in last. Browsing the shelves, she finds the third book of a trilogy she'd been looking for. She wanders around the rest of the shop and picks up a coffee mug with an RCA Victor dog logo imprinted on it, thinking it would make a nice pencil holder next to the register in Murray's shop. Not finding anything else, Delaney pays for her two items — a total of $2.50 — and leaves.

The early afternoon sun feels good and she decides to walk the extra few blocks to The Office to check for mail before going home. She's glad to see Carol working.

"Oh, my goodness," Carol says, "don't you look terrific!"

Delaney smiles at her. "Thanks."

As she puts her key in the box, she is aware that Carol is watching her. Reaching inside to remove the envelope, she looks back at Carol who looks away and starts tidying up the counter. Delaney looks quickly at the envelope and drops it into her purse.

"Bye, Carol," she says, over her shoulder. She's anxious to get home, open the envelope and go online to price the value of her gold chain.

Thirty-Four

The smell of ink and newsprint hangs heavy in the air of the Times-Herald office when Luella pushes the door open and walks in. The grimy, aged appearance of the building, inside and out, makes Luella wonder if the newspaper was born here. An overhead fluorescent bulb illuminates a color scheme of various shades of drab grey from the old metal filing cabinets to the pitted linoleum floor. A computer monitor on the metal-edged Formica countertop looks completely out of place.

"Good afternoon, Ma'am. May I help you?" asks a young man who appears from behind the computer.

"Why yes, I hope so," Luella says. "I'm trying to find some information about a fire that occurred in Vallejo many years ago. If your newspaper wrote an article about it, I'd like to obtain a copy."

"Most of that information is available online now," he says, "but since you're here, I'll see if I can help you find what you need. Do you know the date of the fire?"

"January fourth or fifth and it would have been about seventeen years ago. I appreciate your help."

The young man types so quickly, his fingers are a blur on the keyboard. He clicks the mouse with equal proficiency and Luella watches the expression on his face as he looks at the screen in front of him. She steels herself in anticipation of what she knows will come.

"I do have a short article here," he says, "from the January fifth edition that year. I'm not sure if it's what you're looking for." He turns the monitor around, so Luella can see the screen.

Vallejo Woman Dies in Fire

Authorities have identified the body of a woman killed in a house fire on Bethel Drive as Doris Leanne Tanner, age 39. Preliminary examination indicates the cause of her death was smoke inhalation. The blaze was reported by a neighbor at about 3 a.m. Two other family members, also living in the residence, were able to escape with minor injuries. Fire investigators say the fire appears to have started in the living room and was most likely caused by a frayed electrical cord igniting a dry Christmas tree. Due to the proximity of neighboring structures, three engines responded. Investigators found no evidence of a smoke detector in the home. It is estimated the fire caused $175,000 damage to the 1,800 square foot structure. The American Red Cross is providing temporary shelter to Mrs. Tanner's husband, Keith, and their daughter, Elizabeth Ann.

Luella looks at the young man with tears in her eyes. She tries to speak but is unable to. When he asks if she wants him to print her a copy, she can only nod. He turns the monitor back toward himself and places a dusty tissue box on the counter.

"Would you also have an obituary notice for the victim of the fire?" Luella asks, her voice shaking as she reaches for a tissue.

"Just a moment and I'll check."

Luella dries her eyes and takes a deep breath.

After a few clicks of the mouse, he says, "The obituary ran five days later. I'll print a copy of this for you as well. No charge."

"You're so very kind. Thank you." Luella offers a tentative smile and a wave as she walks out the door, clutching the two pieces of paper in her hand.

Back at her apartment, Luella sits down at the table to consult with Harold. Wringing her hands in her lap, she looks at his kind face and the eyes that held hers for so many years. Her tears begin to flow.

"Oh, honey, don't mind me. I've been cryin' most of the day," she says, wiping her eyes with the back of her hand. "I think I've got this siren problem figured out, but I just don't know how to break all this to Delaney. I don't even know what her mother has told her about how her grandmother died. And what's happened to her grandfather? I can't find him. You'd think all those years of social work would have stiffened me up but look at me. I'm a mess. I wish I could talk to that girl's mother." Luella puts her elbows on the table, heaves a sigh and rests her head in her hands. She is quiet for a moment. "Okay, Harold. All right. I hear you. I will tell Delaney what I've found. Maybe it will be helpful — at least the part about the sirens." Luella picks up Harold's picture and holds it in her hands. "You know, it feels like you're still here with me — listening, understanding, comforting. I love you my dear."

Luella offers a prayer for strength and compassion. She puts the little velvet bag containing the rose quartz bracelet into her purse and picks up the two copies from the newspaper office. Before she can change her mind, she walks down to the carport and backs her Taurus out of its spot. She wants to find Delaney.

Thirty-Five

Luella pulls into Delaney's driveway and parks behind the VW. When Delaney answers her knock, Luella sees immediately that she's been crying.

"Oh, child. What's got you so upset?" Luella puts her arm around Delaney and lets herself in.

"This note was in my mailbox," Delaney says, handing it to Luella. She waits, pacing, while Luella reads it.

"Have you called the officer yet?"

"No. I just opened it before you got here. How did he even find me? I'm not sure what to do. I'd have to go next door to use Murray's phone."

"Or, we could go back to my place and you could use mine," Luella offers. "What do you think he might want to talk to you about?"

"Probably my mother. I wish she'd just leave me alone. I don't want you to have to drive all the way back to Oakland just so I can use your phone. Would you go next door with me?"

"Of course I will. You know I'll help you any way I can."

Delaney lets herself into the laundry room and knocks on Murray's kitchen door. Luella is right behind her.

When Murray opens the door, he waves them in. Delaney introduces him to Luella.

"Luella," he says, taking her hand in both of his, "it's such a pleasure to meet you. Delaney has told me how much she appreciates your friendship."

"Likewise, Murray," Luella says. "You've done this young lady a good turn fixing up that little place for her."

"I hope you don't mind, Murray. I asked Luella to come over with me while I use the phone. I think I need a little moral support."

"What's going on, hon? Anything I can do to help?" he asks.

Delaney hands him the note. "I'll bet it has something to do with my mother. I never told you but she's one of those women who get beat up by abusive boyfriends all the time and then go back for more. It's a huge part of the reason why I left home when I did. I'm sorry to have to bother you with all this, Murray."

"No apologies necessary. Help yourself to the phone. Luella and I will be right here."

Delaney takes a deep breath and dials the number on the business card. A male voice answers.

"Barnes."

"Officer Barnes? Hi. I'm Delaney Moran." She feels Luella's hand lightly rest on her shoulder.

"Hey, Delaney. Thank you for calling me. I wanted to let you know that your mother is in the hospital. She's recovering from a fall and is expected to be discharged home in a couple of days. I should tell you that she didn't want me to contact you. The reason I did is that her doctor says she'll need someone to stay with her for a week or two and we don't know of anyone else who might be available."

Delaney pulls out a kitchen chair and sits down, twirling the phone cord around her finger.

"Are you still there?"

"I don't know if I can do that."

"Would you mind thinking about this overnight and calling me back tomorrow morning?"

Delaney hesitates, then sighs. "I can call you back tomorrow morning but my thinking about it all night isn't going to change the way she lives. There are a lot of things I'm sure you don't know about her."

Murray pours a cup of coffee and sets it on the table.

"I've got to go Officer Barnes. I'll talk to you tomorrow."

"Thanks Delaney," Nick replies.

"I knew it would eventually come to something like this. I should have moved farther away, and I would have if I'd had the money or someplace to stay. He said she fell but that's probably the story she told the police. I'll bet it's true, though, that she told the officer not to contact me. The last time I saw her, when I moved out, she said she never wanted to see me again. Same here. Trust me," Delaney says as she reaches for the cup of coffee.

Murray gestures to Luella, pulling out the other chair at the table. Luella nods and sits down next to Delaney.

"Child, sometimes people say things when they're angry that they regret later. It's just human nature is all. If your mother did regret what she said, she wouldn't have known where you are, to reach out to you."

Delaney runs her fingers through her hair. "You don't understand. It's not like we had one big blow-up," she explains, "My whole childhood was spent watching her go through one bad relationship after another. It was like she had a sickness or an addiction. She'd wind up getting hit and then always blame herself afterward. I got tired of her bruises and her apologies to these jerks. The last straw was when one of them tried to grab me."

"Delaney, as I've told you before, your mother is not alone in her ways. Some women get caught up in that cycle of abuse and can't see their way clear to get out of it without professional help."

"I've never understood men who behave like that; can't control themselves. Aside from that, I haven't told you how much I've missed not seeing my own daughter after her mother took her away." Murray leans against the counter, his arms folded across his chest. "I have no idea where either of them is. Luella might be right that your mother may have had some regrets."

"Have you ever tried to search for your daughter on the Internet?" Delaney asks.

"No. I've thought about it. There's probably a little part of me that's worried about what I might find."

"I'd be happy to help you, Murray, if you decide that's what you want to do," Delaney offers.

"Speaking of deciding what to do, you've got a big cloud of uncertainty looming over your pretty little head, child," Luella says, smoothing Delaney's hair back.

Luella's touch brings on a rush of emotion. Delaney's

eyes well up. Murray rips off a paper towel and hands it to her, patting her on the shoulder.

"You've both been so nice to me," Delaney says, trying to smile. "I'm so glad that you're my friends." She finishes her coffee and stands. Murray takes the cup from her.

"Whatever you need, Delaney, you just let us know. We're here to help you however we can."

"I think I need to go home and wash my face, for starters. Thanks for letting me use your phone, Murray. Guess I'll have to use it again in the morning." She gives Murray a quick hug.

"No problem, hon and if you need transportation anywhere, we can take care of that too."

As Luella follows Delaney out the back door, Murray touches her arm and speaks in a low voice just above a whisper. "I'm glad she has you in her life, Luella."

"Likewise, Murray. We'll get her through this, don't you worry," she says with a wink.

Thirty-Six

While Delaney washes her face and freshens up, Luella fills a mug with water and puts it in the microwave.

"Are you sure you won't join me in a cup of tea?" Luella asks.

"No thanks. I just had coffee over there."

Luella pulls the velvet bag out of her purse and sets it on the table.

"What's this?" Delaney asks when she returns to the room.

"A small thank you from me to you. You can open it while I fix my tea, if you like."

"Cool bag," Delaney says, opening the gift inside. "A bracelet! Oh, Luella, you didn't have to do this." She slips it over her wrist and wraps both arms around Luella in a hug.

"Before you squeeze the stuffing out of me, let me tell you it's made from rose quartz and there's a little card about it in the bag. I'm so grateful to have my Mary bracelet back, I wanted to give you a bracelet, too." Luella brings her tea over to the table.

Delaney reads the card and looks at Luella. "It says rose quartz promotes emotional healing. Huh. I guess we'll see if it works. That's sweet of you. Thanks."

"I'm glad we came back to your place for a little girl talk, because I have a confession to make to you."

Delaney looks at her intently. Something in Luella's face makes her stomach begin to tighten. She sits on the edge of the futon.

"Okay. Go ahead."

"First, let me lay my excuses on the table. Mostly, I did what I did because I want to help you." Luella pauses to take a sip of her tea. "You are a smart and beautiful young woman and it was my hope that by using my skills as a social worker, I could help you uncover the reason for your fear of sirens and help you resolve it. Granted, I'm no doctor but I figured with a bit of concerted effort, we might be able to get to the bottom of this. Are you with me so far?"

Delaney nods, still feeling uncomfortable and not sure where this is going. She shifts her position and crosses her ankles tightly together.

"I took the liberty of researching some public records to see if I could uncover anything in your past that might explain how that fear was originally triggered."

"Wait. You *what*? What do you mean 'anything in my past'?" Delaney doesn't try to hide the irritation in her voice.

"Now honey, these are public records, you know, things like newspapers, birth certificates, that sort of thing. It's information anyone can look for."

Delaney stands and folds her arms across her chest. "You just went off and started looking stuff up without my permission? Seriously?"

Luella rises too and empties her cup in the sink. "Oh dear. I can see you're upset right now. This is bad timing for this conversation. I'm sorry. I was just trying to be helpful. Darn it — sometimes I get in my own way."

Something in the way Luella looks at her when she reaches for her purse softens Delaney a bit.

"It's just that I feel like some insect caught in a spider's web; like I'm trapped or cornered or something. I can't think right now." Delaney sighs. "Sorry. I just need you to go. I've got a lot I need to figure out." She opens the door for Luella and looks down, avoiding eye contact.

"Honey let's give this a little time. I'm sorry I've upset you. You know my number. All you have to do is call." Luella steps through the door and closes it behind her.

Leaning against the back of the door, Delaney waits until she hears Luella's car back out of the driveway and pull away. Hoisting her bag over her shoulder, she steps outside, taking a deep breath of fresh air. She has no idea where she's going as she walks down the street, her mind elsewhere. The mere thought of returning to her mother's house makes her feel as though she might suffocate.

She pauses in her walk to watch a miniature dust devil swirl along the curb, collecting and spinning bits of trash in its tiny vortex; a metaphor for her state of mind as she tries to sort out her thoughts about her friendship with Luella. She doesn't make friends easily and felt she could trust her. Now she isn't so sure.

Daylight is beginning to fade when the smell of hamburgers grilling pulls her inside Buster's, several blocks from home. She orders fries and a vanilla shake and sits down at a booth where someone had left a copy of the local weekly paper. Scanning the pages as she picks at her fries, a photo of three middle-aged black women from a church group catches her eye. Delaney doesn't read the article, but one of the women reminds her of Luella. She becomes aware that she's fingering the bracelet on her wrist. Closing the paper and pushing it aside, she gets up and tosses her trash in the bin.

Walking home under the light of a full moon, Delaney knows one thing for certain. Feeling this way about Luella doesn't make her happy.

Thirty-Seven

Luella senses Harold's eyes following her as she paces back and forth in front of the table. Glancing down, she sees the effect her shoes are having on the nap of the carpet and she drops into a chair.

"Oh, Harold. I've made such a mess of things. Maybe Delaney is right. Maybe I should have minded my own business. I was just trying to help that girl with her trouble, is all."

Maisey puts her front paws up on the edge of Luella's chair.

"Come here," Luella says, lifting the cat into her lap. "How is it you always know when I need a hug? Sometimes I think you animals are wiser than we are." Maisey settles herself and Luella massages the back of her head, behind the ears.

Why didn't I just back off after she talked to the officer? I should have known that call would have upset her. That girl has too much going on right now and all I did was add to her burden. Maisey narrows her eyes and purrs under Luella's hand. *Should I try to contact the officer? What was his name, Burns? Or, what about Murray? Maybe I should talk to Murray. He seems to genuinely care about Delaney. I'm sure he'd like to see her be able to overcome these panic attacks or whatever they are. Yeah, that's it. Murray and I could team up on this. We're probably the only people she has.* She feels Harold's stern gaze.

"All right. Never mind then. I know what you're thinking. I should just wait until she calls me. I suppose you're right. You usually are. Sometimes, when I look at you, your tender face becomes a mirror and for a moment I see myself as you could always see me."

Luella absentmindedly puts Maisey back down on the floor and then fusses about for a few minutes in her tidy kitchen. She decides to go downstairs to see if she can find a movie that will take her mind off Delaney. Not likely, but she'll try.

Thirty-Eight

For a disturbing moment, Delaney sees her mother's haggard face when she looks in the mirror. Her early morning shower didn't wash away the evidence of a sleepless night. Even her freshly shampooed hair seems to fall flat when she blows it dry. Distracted, she has trouble deciding what to wear and finally settles on a teal long-sleeved top overlaid with a small black ivy print and her best jeans.

What if it was really an accident? Maybe her fall didn't have anything to do with one of her jerk boyfriends. Delaney applies mascara and reaffirms the determination she woke with, to comply with the officer's request, visit her mother and put this behind her.

Murray is in the kitchen when she lets herself in. His nod and smile give her the encouragement she needs as she takes a deep breath and reaches for the phone.

Nick is speaking with another officer in the briefing room when his cell phone rings.

"Officer Barnes? This is Delaney Moran. I hope I'm not calling too early."

"Not at all, Delaney."

"I've decided I'm willing to visit my mother in the hospital today. Whether or not I can help her after she's released will depend on how she reacts when she sees me. Does that sound fair enough?"

"It certainly does. What time is good for you?" Nick asks.

"Around noon, if that's alright."

"Should be fine. We'll touch base after. Your mother is at Kaiser in Vallejo. They were moving her to a different room so check in at the information desk when you arrive. Thanks, Delaney."

As soon as he ends the call, he dials Liz's doctor.

"Nick Barnes, here, Benicia PD. I thought I'd better alert you that Liz Tanner's daughter is planning on stopping by the hospital to visit her around noon today. From what I know about their relationship, it's a bit strained so Liz won't be expecting her. This is the only relative we're aware of and she may or may not be able to help Liz for a couple of weeks after her release. Looks like it will depend on how the visit goes."

"Thanks Nick. I'm going to be over there to clear another patient for discharge. I'll make it a point to be in the vicinity of Liz's room around that time, so I'll drop in to check the weather. Let's hope for a peaceful reunion."

Murray gestures to his coffee pot and raises his eyebrows. Delaney declines.

"She's at Kaiser Hospital, Murray."

"Since it's Tuesday, I'd be happy to give you a ride if you'd like."

"That would be great," she says. "I'd really appreciate it."

"I know a good little cafe over there, down by the water. Can I take you to lunch after your visit?"

"Sure, if you can keep me from throwing myself off the pier after seeing my mother," she says, managing a grin. "I'd like to call Luella first."

"Go right ahead." Murray disappears into the store.

Luella picks up the phone on the second ring.

"Luella? I want to say…"

"Delaney? I am so very sorry."

"No, I'm sorry. I was rude."

"Oh child, I'm the one should know better. I don't blame you for being upset."

Delaney hears the shakiness in Luella's voice. "Do you think we could meet this morning? I told the officer I'd go see my mother at noon, but I'd like to talk to you first."

"Of course, honey."

"How about the Bean?"

"Okay, give me an hour. Should I pick you up?"

"No, I'll just see you there. I need the walk. Thanks, Luella."

Delaney cradles the receiver and finds Murray red-stickering a stack of CDs for clearance. He looks over his shoulder at her.

"Everything okay?"

"We'll see. I'll be back by 11:30. Thanks again for offering to take me."

"You bet."

Thirty-Nine

Luella quickens her pace as she approaches the coffee shop. Delaney is sitting at a corner table and doesn't look up when the door opens. She appears to be deep in thought. An untouched blueberry muffin sits on a plate in front of her.

As Luella nears the table, Delaney pushes her chair back and stands to welcome her with a hug that is gratefully returned.

"Luella, I'm so happy to see you. Can I get you some tea? Did you have breakfast?"

"I could use a cup of tea. Chamomile, please. That muffin looks good but why do they make them so big?"

"I'll get your tea and a knife. We can share the muffin. I'm not as hungry as I thought I was."

While Delaney moves toward the counter, Luella settles herself into a chair with a deep sigh. Uncomfortably warm in the morning buzz of the coffee shop, she removes her hat and shrugs off her navy sweater. *Don't blow it this time. Pace yourself. Let her lead the conversation.*

Delaney returns and sets a cup and teapot on the table.

"I'm really sorry about last night. I know you're trying to help."

"The blame is all mine. I was wrong to bring that up when you were confronted with your mother being in the hospital. I should have had more sense," Luella says, fussing with a packet of sugar.

Delaney cuts the muffin in half and pushes the plate and a napkin toward Luella.

"You said something about researching public records. Did you find anything I should know about before I go and see my mother?"

"Well, I may have." Luella pinches off a bite-sized piece of muffin. "All those years of workin' my caseload, I just slipped back into my old routine. To you, it probably seems like I was snooping around and to me it felt like I was problem-solving."

"I know. I thought about that last night when I was trying to fall asleep."

"When we first met, you told me you didn't have any grandparents. Were you referring to both sides of your family?" Luella asks.

Delaney pokes at her half of the muffin with her fork. "I told you what my mother always told me. First of all, my father left before I was born so I don't know anything about him or his parents. As far as my mother's side is concerned, she told me her parents had both died in an automobile accident in Chicago, just before I was born. Like I said, there weren't any aunts, uncles or cousins, either."

Luella takes a sip of her tea. "Delaney, I believe you also said that telling the truth wasn't your mother's strong point. Is that correct, child?"

"Yes. She lies all the time," Delaney says, putting her fork down.

"Well, this is a difficult conversation to have right before you're going to go visit her in the hospital. Are you sure you want me to continue?" The espresso machine hisses in the background as more customers drift in.

Delaney nods. Luella reaches over and squeezes her hand.

"Let me tell you what I found out and I'll start from the beginning," Luella says. "I went to the Office of Vital Records to look up your birth certificate. I'm guessing this is a document you've never seen."

"You're right. My mother would have had a copy though, wouldn't she?"

"Most likely. She would have needed one to enroll you in school. Anyway, according to your birth certificate, both of your parents were very young when you were born. Your mother was only seventeen and your father eighteen. Your mother gave you your father's last name. Since she was underage, she would have needed her parents' permission in order to marry him."

"But they were both dead," Delaney interjects.

"You best eat your half of that muffin, hon. You're going to need your strength this morning."

Delaney takes a bite as four people try to squeeze around the table next to theirs. She and Luella slide their chairs over as far as they can. Luella leans over the table, lowers her voice and continues.

"I didn't look up any further information about your father, Marty Moran. Instead, I thought I would look for your mother's birth certificate to find out the names of her parents. Now, to do that, I guessed she might have been born in Solano County and maybe that's not correct. Also, your mother's name, Elizabeth Ann Tanner, is not a particularly uncommon name."

"Did you find her birth certificate?" Delaney tucks a strand of hair behind her ear.

"I believe so. Is your mother's birthday October thirteenth?" Luella asks.

"Yes, it is."

A cell phone rings loudly at the next table.

"All right then. Since you're done eating, would you like to go out to my car? It's getting kind of noisy and crowded in here."

Delaney nods, gathers their dishes and puts them in the tub on the cart.

Outside, Luella puts her hat back on. "Would you like a ride over to the hospital?"

"Thanks, but Murray offered to drive me since the store is closed today. He wants to take me to lunch after the visit. He knows a place near there."

"He seems like a good person, Delaney. It eases my mind a bit to know you have him close by."

Luella gestures toward her car, parked around the corner. "I was lucky enough to find a shady spot this morning, so we can sit inside." When they reach the car, Luella opens the door for Delaney. "Give me just a minute and I'll put our windows down."

Luella slides her driver's seat back to allow more room for her purse on her lap.

"The birth certificate I found was for an Elizabeth Ann Tanner born on October thirteenth here in Solano County. Her mother's name is Doris Leanne and her father's name is Keith Wade. They were also young parents when your mother was born. Doris was eighteen and Keith was twenty."

Delaney shifts in her seat. "Doris and Keith. I never knew their names before. This is crazy. Did you check the records in Chicago for their deaths?"

"I checked the Social Security Death Index which covers the whole country. When I typed in your grandmother's name it found a match for a death that occurred here in Vallejo on January fifth, less than a month before you were born."

"Wait a minute. What?" Delaney runs her hand through her hair. "In Vallejo? From an automobile accident? What about my grandfather?"

"When I typed his name into the index, no match came up at all. I tried it twice to be sure."

"So, what does that mean?"

"There's a possibility your grandfather could still be alive." Luella reaches over and takes hold of Delaney's hand.

Delaney looks out the window. A young couple is pushing an empty stroller down the sidewalk. Their little girl is being carried on the father's shoulders, where she rests her chin on top of his head. Pulling her hand away, Delaney fumbles in her purse. As soon as she lowers her head, tears begin to stream down her cheeks. "Wow." She turns toward Luella and wipes her face with a crumpled napkin. "I don't know what to say. All this time, I've never known what it would be like to have a grandfather and I might actually have one? He must not even know I exist, then. Why did my mother have to lie to me?"

"She must have had her reasons, right or wrong."

Luella takes two pieces of folded paper out of her purse and holds them. "Delaney, honey, I'd like to show you what I found but this isn't going to be easy for you. Do you understand what I'm saying?"

Delaney takes a deep breath. Her hands are clenched in her lap as Luella unfolds the papers. When Luella asks if she's ready, she gives a quick nod.

"This is a copy of an article from the *Times-Herald*. You'll notice the date at the top. This other sheet is a copy of your grandmother's obituary notice that ran in the same paper a few days later." She hands both to Delaney.

Luella takes a packet of tissues from her purse and pulls one out for herself as Delaney reads the article.

"Oh, Luella." Delaney begins to sob. They share the tissues and in the cramped space of the car, lean over and put their arms around each other. Luella finds herself crying, too.

"If she was still alive, she'd be right about my age," she tells Delaney "and she would be so very proud of you." She pulls Delaney close and strokes her hair.

"Will you help me try to find my grandfather?" Delaney asks, her voice small and tight. "That must have been so horrible for him — to lose his wife in a fire. He must have known his daughter was pregnant. Why did he disappear? I don't understand what happened."

"I would be honored to try to help you find him," Luella

says, "but understand that even if we do, all your questions might not be answered."

"Delaney, there is something else you should know. Studies have been done that show a fetus hears sounds after thirty weeks of gestation. If these dates are correct, your mother would have been about thirty-six weeks along with you on the morning of the fire, when three engines responded with all of their sirens blaring."

"So, what you're saying is that I could have been scared by those sirens before I was even born? Really? That seems so crazy, but I guess it kinda makes sense. I remember *always* being afraid of sirens, even when I was very little."

"Well, maybe now you know the reason why."

Luella wipes a smear of mascara from Delaney's cheek. "This has been quite a morning for you and it's not over yet." She checks her watch. "I think I'd better run you home, so you can freshen up a bit before you go over there with Murray." She turns her key in the ignition. "Remember, your mother isn't going to know that you've figured any of this out."

Forty

Delaney is tense on her way to the hospital. Her fingers twist the shoulder strap of her bag and she feels Murray glance over at her every so often. She directs her gaze out her window to avoid conversation, grateful that Murray seems to understand. Several minutes go by before he pulls the VW into a parking space in the visitor lot and turns off the ignition.

"Are you going to be okay, Delaney?" he asks.

"Yeah. I think so, Murray. Are you going to wait in the car?"

"No, if it's all the same to you, I'll come inside and find a seat in the waiting room on your mother's floor. That way I'll be close by if you need me," he says.

Delaney leans over the gear shift and gives Murray a quick hug. "You're the best, Murray. Let's go get this over with, one way or the other."

They stop at the information desk in the lobby before riding the elevator to the third floor. A sign directs them to the waiting area.

"I'll be right here," Murray nods toward a seat, as he reaches for a magazine.

Delaney finds a nearby restroom, runs her brush through her hair and puts on a little lip gloss. Heaving a big sigh and straightening her posture, she heads down the hall to find her mother's room.

Gently pushing open the door, she steps quietly past the first empty bed and peers around the curtain. She is not prepared for what she sees. Liz's face is wrapped in bandages. Her eyes are open. The tip of her nose and her mouth are barely visible.

Delaney clears her throat. "Um, Mom?"

Liz's eyes turn in her direction. "Delaney. What did you do to your hair?" The voice is somewhat muffled but recognizable. And critical.

Delaney approaches the bed cautiously. She starts to reach for her mother's hand and pulls back.

"My hair? What did you do to your face?"

"I fell," Liz says, haltingly. "I'm glad you're here. I need you to do . . ."

"What, Mom?"

Liz speaks slowly and carefully, without moving her jaw. "I need you to go down to the jail." She pauses to take a breath. "Ask if you can post bail to get Jeff out. Do you understand?" Liz looks directly into Delaney's eyes and waits for an answer.

"Who is Jeff?" Delaney lowers her voice. She hears footsteps and sees someone in a white coat pass by her mother's room.

Liz points to the water cup with a straw on the bedside tray. Delaney picks it up and gently pushes the tip of the straw between her mother's lips. Liz takes a sip and with a wave of her hand indicates she doesn't want anymore.

"He's my boyfriend." Liz rests for a moment before continuing. "He shouldn't be in jail. He didn't hit me." She sighs. "I fell. That's what happened. I need him to take care of me when I get out. Could you go do that for me?"

"Mom, are you telling me the truth about falling?" Delaney asks.

"Are you accusing me of *lying*?" Liz raises her voice and the effort makes her cough. She stiffens her arms and tries to pull herself into a sitting position.

"You lied to me about your parents, didn't you? Maybe you should ask your father for help."

"What? Get the hell out of here you little bitch! Nurse!" Liz yells and pushes the red call button.

"You are still so messed up," Delaney says, her own voice shaking. She turns to walk out of the room and almost bumps into Liz's doctor as he enters.

"Get her out!" Liz yells.

"I'm already leaving." Delaney walks down the hall without looking back.

In the waiting room, the TV is on with the volume low. Murray sets his magazine aside and gets up from his chair.

"I heard a little commotion a minute ago. I'm guessing your visit didn't go well?"

"Pretty much the way I expected it would. She hasn't changed a bit. Let's get out of here."

They're waiting for the elevator when Liz's doctor approaches and introduces himself. He asks if he might speak to Delaney privately for a moment. They step back into the waiting room.

Delaney folds her arms across her chest and speaks first. "I'm her daughter. An only child, thankfully. Were her injuries really caused by a fall?"

"Well, yes and no. When she was brought into the ER, we noticed other facial injuries that appear to have been suffered a day or two before her fall. Has your mother been the victim of abuse in the past?"

"Yes, she has, for as long as I can remember. She seems to thrive on it. That's why I had to move out. I couldn't watch it anymore. She hasn't seen me in over a year and she just asked me to go down to the jail and bail out her current boyfriend. I'm sorry, doctor. There's nothing I can do for her."

"Most likely, we'll have to discharge her to a rehab facility for a short while if she has no one to help her at home."

"Then I guess that's the way it has to be," Delaney responds with a shrug. "I'm sorry."

Forty-One

Delaney walks back to join Murray at the elevator. When they reach the main lobby, she points to a pay phone on the wall.

"I need to give Officer Barnes a call. Would you mind waiting a minute?"

"Not at all. Take your time."

When Nick answers, Delaney tells him about the conversation with her mother and the doctor.

"I appreciate the effort Delaney. I know it wasn't easy. The fact of the matter is that Jeff is serving time for violating his probation. He's not eligible for release on bail. Furthermore, if Liz cooperates with the district attorney's office, he'll be looking at more time for charges related to domestic violence."

"Don't hold your breath. I'm sure she won't press charges against him. This has been her pattern for a very long time," Delaney says. "It's what I grew up with. One more thing — she lies. Just thought you should know." She hangs up the phone.

"Hungry?" Murray asks as they leave the building.

"Yes, I am. I didn't think I'd want to eat after seeing her but suddenly I'm starving."

"Good. Me too. Happy Skillet here we come."

Delaney calls Luella from Murray's phone as soon as they get back.

"Let's do this," Luella says, "Why don't I come over and pick you up in a little while and bring you back to my place. You can pack your pajamas and we'll have us a sleepover. That'll give us plenty of time to talk."

"Only if you let me treat you to dinner," Delaney insists.

"Deal. I've got to run some errands first. Does five o'clock sound alright?"

"Sure, that's perfect. See you then. Thanks, Luella."

Murray told Delaney that Julian had left a message for her on his machine.

She dials his number next, smiling at the thought of hearing his voice.

"Julian? Hi, it's Delaney."

"Hey. Been thinking about you. Got time to meet for a quick cup before I go to work?"

"Yeah, sure. The Bean?"

"Yup. Thirty minutes?"

"See you there."

Delaney turns to Murray and thanks him for letting her use the phone.

"Are you feeling okay?" Murray asks.

"I'll be fine, Murray. I'm glad you were there this morning. I don't know what I would have done without you."

"Glad to help. Anytime."

Back at her place, Delaney changes into a bright blue tank top. Rooting around in her dresser drawer, she finds a small silver pendant on a sheer blue ribbon and ties it around her neck. She slips the new bracelet Luella gave her over her wrist, combs her hair and heads down the street to meet Julian.

"You look good," he says and gives her a quick kiss on the cheek when she walks in a few minutes later. "You smell good too."

Delaney smiles.

He's already ordered her coffee and brings their two mugs over to the seats in the window, where they'd first met.

"I'm glad you called," Delaney admits. "So much has happened, Julian. This morning was crazy!"

"What's going on?"

Settling herself on the stool, she tells him about the research Luella had done and what she'd learned about her grandparents. She also tells him a police officer from Benicia tracked her down and about visiting her mother in the hospital. He listens attentively.

"Wow. It's like your life story has been rewritten. So, where does all this leave you now?" he asks, running his fingers through his hair.

"Well, if I ever had any doubt in my mind about whether or not my relationship with my mom could be repaired, I don't anymore. I'm so over it. She's beyond hope. In a way, it's kinda liberating to feel positively sure about that. I gave her one last chance and she blew it."

"What about your grandfather? Are you going to try to find him?"

"I'd really like to. Besides my mother, I've never had any other family. I'm still trying to get used to the idea of having a grandfather after I thought he was dead all these years."

"Aren't you wondering what his reaction will be if you do find him?"

"Let's just say I hope he's not like his daughter. There must have been some bad blood between the two of them for her to basically have wished him dead." Delaney downs the rest of her coffee. "I'm going to see Luella tonight and maybe she can help me figure out a strategy for where to go from here."

"Hey, speaking of tonight, I'd better get going. I've got to help set up for 'Alternating Current'. This is the first time I've seen a group with so much lighting equipment it arrives in its own truck. I didn't realize it was almost four already."

"I'm sorry. I hope you're not late. Guess I just needed to talk."

He took her hands in his. "There's nobody I would rather have been with. Call me tomorrow and let me know what you've figured out. Oh, and hey, if you need someone who looks like a random guy to check out a possible grandpa or anything, I'm your man," he says with a nod. "Gotta go. Call me."

"I will. Thanks for the coffee."

Julian pulls her close and kisses her lightly on the lips before he hustles out the door. Delaney shoulders her purse and walks back up the street to pack an overnight bag, re-playing that kiss over and over in her mind.

Forty-Two

"Are you ready for some girl time?" Luella asks as she backs the car out of Delaney's driveway.

"I'm ready for a stiff drink but I guess that's out," Delaney says with a sigh.

"I'll bet you are. Well, we could get some drunken noodles at a Thai restaurant if you want," Luella says, chuckling. "Or, I know a place with tasty Chinese food in Oakland."

"Chinese sounds good. Don't forget, it's my treat."

After threading her way through rush hour traffic, Luella parks in front of The Noodle House near downtown.

"This restaurant meets all of my criteria for eating out: good food, reasonable prices and it's quiet enough to carry on a conversation even when they're busy."

Luella and Delaney are shown to a booth in the back with big black vinyl seats and a plexiglass-covered table.

"This place has the best soup. They bring it on a little burner that keeps it warm while you eat."

Delaney closes her menu. "Perfect. Let's order some egg rolls, too."

Luella places their order, then she looks Delaney directly in the eye, her hands folded in front of her.

"So, tell me, how did it go?"

Delaney opens her napkin and smooths it over her lap.

"I tried not to think about what you told me, especially after I saw how bandaged up she was. I only went because I felt some sort of obligation, I guess, to give her one more chance, to see if maybe she was finally ready to pull herself together."

Tea and egg rolls are brought to the table and Luella is grateful for the brief interlude to compose her thoughts.

"Was your mother alert? Could she speak?" Luella asks.

Delaney swirls some hot mustard into her little bowl of sweet red sauce.

"Careful hon, that stuff is pretty spicy. You don't want to burn your tongue."

Delaney picks up half an egg roll and stabs it into the sauce.

"Good. Maybe it'll clear my head. It was so strange, Luella. She hadn't seen me in over a year and she acted like it was yesterday. She expected me to fall right in and do what she wanted me to." Taking a bite, she reaches for her glass of water. "She straight up asked me to go see if I could bail out that jerk. Can you believe it?"

Luella's eyes met Delaney's. She shook her head. "She's living in a separate reality — playing her life with a whole different hand of cards. Unfortunately, that won't change until she decides she's ready to do things differently and apparently, even from a hospital bed, she hasn't reached that point yet. Some women don't until it's too late. I've seen it happen too many times."

The waitress sets a large bowl of steaming soup in front of them.

"Luella, the first thing she said was 'what did you do to your hair?'" Delaney says, her voice beginning to quiver.

"That's because she can't see outside herself, Delaney. I'm sorry for her and the years she is wasting. I'm afraid her loss has become one of my greatest blessings." Luella reaches over and squeezes Delaney's hand. Her squeeze is returned.

Later, at Luella's apartment, Delaney pulls a small sandwich bag out of her duffel bag and offers Maisey a treat. Maisey takes it from her hand and then nuzzles her leg. Luella notices this from the kitchen and smiles.

"I always keep some chicken treats on hand for Lyric and Melody, so I thought I'd bring Maisey a few for putting up with me."

"Have you been thinking about your grandparents?" Luella asks.

"I have. A lot. One of the things I'd like to do is visit my grandmother's grave. Would you be willing to go with me?"

"Of course, child. Whenever you're ready."

"I've also decided I definitely want to try and find my grandfather. If we can find him and he'll talk to me, maybe he'll have a different side of the story to tell. It feels pretty weird to have lived seventeen years believing what you were told about your family only to find out it was all an outright lie," Delaney says, bending down to scratch Maisey behind her ears.

"Did I hear you say, 'if *we* can find him'?" Luella asks, raising an eyebrow.

"Did I say that?" Delaney answers with a smile. "I'm going to do some searching on the Internet first thing tomorrow, now that you've found out his name. Maybe he'll still be in the area." Delaney shrugs her shoulders. "I wonder what he looks like."

"Ready for some homemade peach cobbler with vanilla ice cream?" Luella sets a casserole dish on a hot pad on her table. The fragrant cobbler is still warm.

"Mmmmm, that smells so good. You're such an amazing cook, Luella. Look at the way that peachy sauce bubbled up around the golden topping. Did your mother teach you?"

"Mostly, I suppose she did," Luella says, dishing up two generous servings of cobbler.

"Like I said, I'm no fancy cook, though. I go for simple recipes that are nourishing and tasty."

Delaney picks up her fork as the ice cream begins to melt.

"This is wonderful, Luella," she says, taking a bite. I don't think I've ever had anything that tasted this good. When I was little, I was lucky to get a cookie out of a package for dessert."

"I'm glad you're enjoying it. That's what makes me happy."

After dessert, they go downstairs to choose a movie. Midway through, Luella notices Delaney has fallen asleep on the loveseat. She covers her with a soft cotton quilt and dims the light.

Arriving back in Vallejo in the morning, they find Murray watering the little cherry tomato plant.

"Hey, what have you girls been up to?" he asks.

"We're on a mission," Luella says, "to find a missing grandpa."

"If you turn him up, I might hire you to find my daughter."

Delaney unlocks her door and Luella follows her inside. She puts two mugs of water in the microwave while she waits for her laptop to boot up. Luella has her eyes on the screen.

"Why does your computer say "Welcome, Webweaver?" she asks.

"Oh, it's the ID I use. I originally chose it because I like spiders."

"Well, I think it suits you. Especially now," Luella adds.

When Delaney enters his name into the search bar, a long list of results for "Keith Wade Tanner" appears. Luella sighs. "It takes a whole lot of patience to do this kind of work," she says, shaking her head.

"Yeah, but it's cheaper than hiring a private investigator. I wish we knew a little more about him, like where he's likely to be or what kind of work he did. Does. Work he *does*," Delaney says, correcting herself, "assuming he's still working."

She fixes tea for herself and Luella and starts clicking on the results, going down the list in order. Luella has a notepad on her lap and a pen in her hand.

They've been squinting at the screen for nearly half an hour before Delaney hits on a link that Luella thinks might be promising. It's a reference to a Keith W. Tanner in a newsletter of the Inlandboatmen's Union, San Francisco Bay chapter and it mentions he and several others were to receive recognition for their years of service to the ferry system. The article doesn't mention his age, specifically, but Luella notes this as a possibility anyway. Delaney continues checking out the other results but finds nothing worthwhile. She looks up the IBU and learns it is the Longshore and Warehouse Union's Maritime Division.

"Luella, if he *is* the right person, how will we know where to find him? Will the ferry company tell us?"

"No, they probably won't. This is where you have to have a little bit of what they call finesse — a way of being able to get information out of people. That's something social workers must do all the time. Sometimes it works and sometimes it doesn't, but I say it's worth a try. You ready to go down to the ferry terminal?"

"I am!" Delaney hops up out of her seat and grabs her purse. "Let's go! Even though we can't be sure this is him, I'm already trying to imagine a rugged, hard-working man whose face has been weathered by the sea over the years."

"Whoa, there. We're not sure yet." Luella says, as she pushes herself up off the futon. "Let's take it easy. You need to follow my lead. We've got to think things through and be careful about our approach."

Delaney wraps her arms around Luella in a big hug. "You're absolutely the best friend anyone could ever have."

Luella squeezes her back. "You best settle down a little bit, child. I don't want you to be too disappointed if we can't find this man or if we do find him, he's not the person we're looking for. Get yourself a sweater or light jacket to bring with you."

Forty-Three

Luella drives into the Washington Street garage at Jack London Square, pulls a parking ticket from the machine and secures a spot on the second level.

"Okay, Miss Dee, follow me. Keep your eyes and ears open," Luella says as she locks the car.

"Are you saying my mouth should be closed?" Delaney asks.

"I didn't say that, did I?" Luella says, patting her on the shoulder. "Remember what I told you, let me do the talking."

Delaney follows, a step behind Luella as she walks toward the Clay Street pier. She's not sure if it's the broad straw hat Luella is wearing or the way she confidently carries herself with purpose in her stride, but she appears to be a woman who won't be questioned. They pass a statue of Jack London and continue on.

"Do you think we'll see him today?"

Luella shrugs. "No way to know yet."

The dock isn't crowded but Delaney imagines that during commute hours and weekends, it must be bustling with activity. Luella steps up to the ticket booth and pays the fare for two adult round-trip tickets to San Francisco for the 2:30 departure. She checks her watch.

"We've got an hour or so to wait. How about an ice cream cone?"

Delaney nods. Perhaps a scoop of ice cream will fill the hollow pit she suddenly feels in her stomach. She turns to Luella.

"I'm not going to know what to say to him."

Luella links her arm through Delaney's and steers her in the direction of the ice cream shop.

"If we do find the right person, I'm hoping to have the chance to meet him first. Let's not forget this will be a surprise to him as well. We don't know how receptive he'll be to the sudden appearance of a granddaughter. We have to ease into this."

"I'm really sorry you didn't have children of your own Luella. You would have been such a good mother."

"Well, thank you for saying so but I don't think a good mother would buy jumbo sugar cones for lunch," she says.

They're walking toward a bench with their ice cream when Luella suddenly hands her cone to Delaney.

"Here, hold this. Go sit tight for a minute."

Luella walks over to a railing by the water where a man in blue coveralls has stopped and set a metal lunch box on the ground. He's black and maybe in his mid-thirties. Delaney watches as he lights a cigarette and looks up when Luella approaches.

Luella has her back to Delaney, and they are too far away for her to overhear their conversation, but she sees the man point across the bay. Luella returns and reclaims her cone just as the mocha fudge ice cream is beginning to drip. The man has picked up his lunch box and is walking down the secured ramp to the ferry.

"Keith doesn't go by his first name," Luella says, sitting down next to her and tidying up her cone with her tongue. "People know him as 'Wade' and he's a deckhand, just like that man I was talking to. He'd wear the same blue coveralls."

Delaney covers her mouth with her hand and swallows.

"You best mind your cone before it drips in your lap."

"Oh my God Luella, you're amazing! Why did he point across the bay?"

"Wade is on the San Francisco side right now. He'll be finishing his shift on the six thirty run to Oakland from Pier 41. Now, before you go getting all excited, just remember that we don't know for sure this is the man we're looking for."

Delaney tries to conjure up an image of what her grandfather might look like but comes up blank. Tall? Short? Facial hair?

Two sea gulls land on the dock not far from them.

"Did you ask that guy how old Wade is?"

One of the gulls bobs his head up and down and begins to inch his way toward Delaney.

"Not in that way." Luella wipes her mouth with a napkin. "This is where the finesse I was telling you about comes in. You have to know just how to apply it and when. I told him I was looking for an IBU member about my age by the name of Tanner. See, Delaney, you have to work it so they draw their own conclusions without you having to lie to get what you want. He looked at me when I asked and maybe he figured I had a brother or some other relative in the union by the way I put the question. He was very nice, and I was grateful he didn't ask me why I was inquiring."

"What would you have said if he did?" Delaney asks, tossing a small piece of her sugar cone to the bird. The other gull squawks.

"Oh, hush yourself," Luella scolds the noisy bird. "That's the other thing. You always need to be ready, just in case. If he'd asked me why, I would have told him I wanted to thank him personally for a kindness he'd done to me and I would have left it right there. You see? That's not far from the truth at all when you think about it, is it?" Luella reaches over and pats Delaney's knee.

After finishing their cones, they poke around a couple of shops before boarding the ferry. Luella settles herself into a forward-facing seat with a sigh.

"I always like a ginger ale when I'm on the water. Settles my stomach."

"I saw the snack bar when we came in. I'll go see if they have one for you. Be right back," Delaney says.

The ferry floor vibrates from the engine noise and the cabin begins to smell of fuel as the ferry slowly pulls away from the dock. Delaney navigates her way around standing passengers and rows of seats as she returns with Luella's drink.

"Here you go — one ginger ale on the rocks. If it's okay with you, I want to wander around the boat and have a look."

"Go right ahead. I'll be here resting my feet," Luella says, toeing off her shoes.

Trying to be discreet while paying attention to what deckhands are doing, Delaney explores the ferry. One of the men briefly makes eye contact with her. She smiles and looks away, trying to picture the faceless grandfather who may be his coworker. She feels unsettled; unsure of what to expect if she meets him. Outside on the deck, Delaney turns her face into the wind, welcoming the occasional spray of salty mist in her face. Taking a deep breath, she draws in the brackish smell of the bay, holding onto the rail as the bow slices through the small whitecaps. The temperature on the water is just cool enough to make her glad she brought her denim jacket.

With the dock at the San Francisco Ferry Building in sight, Delaney returns to the inside cabin where she finds Luella dozing in her seat.

As soon as Delaney sits down beside her, Luella opens her eyes. "Have you ever been to Pier 39?" she asks.

"No. I remember a school field trip to the Exploratorium once, but I've never been to Fisherman's Wharf," Delaney says.

Luella slips her shoes back on. "It's pretty much a tourist trap but we need to kill some time so let's take a walk."

Delaney shrugs.

"We have to pass by it on our way to Pier 41 anyway. We can go pretend we're tourists and have some fun."

Off the ferry, they join a crowd of people walking along The Embarcadero. Luella notices Delaney wrinkling her nose.

"Don't worry yourself. That smell's not coming from a restaurant."

"I sure hope not. What is it?" Delaney asks.

"You'll see in a few minutes."

When they arrive at Pier 39, Luella takes Delaney around to the west side of the pier where she points at the floating platforms below.

"Oh, my God," Delaney says, holding her nose. "Are those seals?"

"Sea lions. They haul themselves up out of the water to sunbathe. Look at the way the color of their coats shines in the sun, almost golden-like. I agree, they don't smell nice but aren't they a magnificent creature? Another example of the Lord's fine handiwork. He keeps everything in balance, right here in our own bay."

Anxious to get away from the smell, Delaney pulls Luella into a hat shop. They take turns trying on different styles, each attempting to outdo the other. Luella is wearing a hat that looks like a birthday cake, complete with candles, when an annoyed saleswoman approaches her.

"May I help you with something?" she asks as Luella catches a glimpse of herself in a mirror.

Luella removes the hat and hands it to the woman.

"No, I don't think so. We were just having a little fun."

Outside, she and Delaney burst into a fit of giggles.

"Luella, if I had a lot of money, I would have bought that hat for you. You looked like a one-woman party!"

"I think my hunger is starting to impair my judgment. We should probably grab a little something before we go back across the bay, otherwise it'll be pretzels and peanuts on the boat."

Delaney points to a chalkboard sign standing on the ground in front of a soup cart a few yards away. The sign reads "Fresh Calm Chowder to go."

"Perfect! Just what we need," Delaney says, laughing at the ironic misspelling. "My treat." They take their cups of chowder and packets of oyster crackers to a bench near the end of the pier. In a matter of minutes, they're joined by a small flock of seagulls; some perching along the rail while others pace impatiently on the ground near their feet.

"Now, see? Would you look at that. We better not give them anything until we're done eating or we might find them crawling up our legs to stick their beaks in our cups. They seem to be pretty aggressive," Luella says, shooing them away with her hand. As if on cue, one seagull jumps up and squats on the edge of their seat where he watches them and waits.

Delaney notices one mottled grey gull who stands apart from the others on the railing. She tosses her last cracker in her direction and the bird catches it neatly.

"I can't remember when I last walked so much in one day," Luella says as they head to Pier 41. "When I find Wade Tanner, I hope he's going to be near a seat where I can plant my bottom while I talk to him. Let's board toward the front of the line. When we get on the boat, you go find yourself a seat, so I'll know where you're going to be. I'll look around a bit and see if I can spot him and then I'll come back and let you know what I find out. I think its best if we aren't seen together, right at first. Okay?"

"You're the boss, Luella. I'm kind of nervous and excited at the same time. If it's him, I won't even know what to say." Delaney nervously twirls a strand of hair around her finger.

"We're not at that bridge yet. I've already asked Jesus to give you strength and guide you through whatever is about to happen. You need not worry, child. Your words will find each other and sort themselves out. Here's your ticket. Let's go get in line."

Forty-Four

As the last few passengers board, Wade Tanner hops from the ferry to the dock to ready the ship for departure. He's looking forward to getting home, popping open a beer and throwing a steak on the barbeque to kick off his weekend. Once the gangplank is secured and the mooring lines are untied, he swings himself aboard, glad to be clear of fumes from the engine. He takes a quick look around to check for passenger safety and sees a boy playing on the staircase to the upper level.

"Hey buddy. We're gonna set sail here. Find your mom or dad and take a seat."

The boy scurries up the stairs. Wade goes to the back of the boat to check the bar area. Folks seem to be settling in with their beverages. The ferry is just pulling away from the dock when his radio crackles to life with a request for a mop-up in the men's head. Johnny, one of the other hands, replies that he'll take care of it. Wade goes upstairs to look around the deck as the ship leaves the San Francisco harbor and gets up to cruising speed.

"Excuse me, sir," a woman's voice says.

Wade turns to see a middle-aged, softly rounded black woman holding onto the railing with one hand, keeping her hat on her head with the other.

"Yes, can I help you?" Wade asks, raising his voice to be heard over the drone of the engine.

"Are you Mr. Tanner?" the woman inquires, looking him directly in the eye with a piercing gaze.

"Yes. I am." He sees her face relax into a hint of a smile.

"Do I know you?" he asks, puzzled.

"Well, you will in a minute. Is there a place we can talk that's less noisy?" Luella asks, straining her voice to be heard.

Wade motions for her to follow him to another area of the sun deck. He steps behind a bulkhead and she comes around next to him.

"Oh, that's much better," she says, lowering herself into a seat. He remains standing.

"I don't believe we've met before," Wade says, wondering where this is leading.

"No, we haven't. My name is Luella Mayfield," she says, as they shake hands. "It's a long story why I'm on this boat today and I see no reason to bore you with the details if you're not the man I'm looking for."

At this, he grins. "Are you going to give me a clue, Miss Mayfield?"

"I'll give you two clues, Mr. Tanner. Do the names Doris and Elizabeth hold any special meaning for you?"

Luella watches his face carefully. His grin fades and his features take on a look of troubled sadness.

"Looks like I may have found the right man," she says, lowering her voice. "I know you're on the clock right now, but can you sit for just a minute?"

Wade quickly scans the deck and lowers himself into a

seat facing her. He runs his fingers over the light stubble on his chin, then leans forward, one hand on each knee.

"Let me tell you right up front, I'm not here about Doris or Elizabeth. The good Lord has seen fit to bless me with the friendship of a fine, young woman who has asked for my help in finding a grandfather she has never known. I certainly understand this must be a shock for you."

Wade feels as though he's suffered a blow to the stomach. He turns his head away, his gaze directed across the bay at nothing, his mind spinning. Luella sees the muscles in his face tighten.

"She would be about seventeen years old, then," he sighs. Turning back to Luella, he asks, "is she with you?"

"Her name is Delaney. Yes, she is aboard this ferry but she's on the lower level. I thought it best not to risk her being hurt if you weren't interested in meeting her so when I saw you come upstairs, I followed you up alone."

"How did you know it was me, Miss Mayfield?"

"Please call me Luella. Before I retired, I was a social worker, so I've had some experience at putting pieces together. I don't want to take up any more of your time while you're working, and I know you probably need some room to wrap your head around this, so here's what I propose. When we dock at Jack London Square, I'm going to tell Delaney I feel like a cup of tea and she and I will go into that coffee shop that's right near the fountain. You can figure we'll be there for nearly an hour. If you'd like to meet her, then please join us. Either way, let me give you my card in case you change your mind later."

Luella crosses off the office number and adds her home number. She gives it to Wade and stands up. "It was nice to meet you Mr. Tanner. Now I know where Delaney got those stunning blue eyes." Luella smiles and holds her hat in place as she steps around the bulkhead into the wind.

Delaney is full of questions when Luella returns to the cabin on the main deck.

"Did you find him Luella?"

"Yes. He's definitely your grandpa."

"What does he look like?"

"Same blue eyes as you, Delaney. Probably six feet tall, grayish hair, good looking and just beginning to show a few lines around his mouth and eyes. Sixty-ish, maybe."

"Am I going to get to meet him?"

"We spoke only briefly, and of course my mention of you came as quite a surprise. I think he'll need at least the rest of our trip across the bay to swallow this. You need to be patient. The ball is in his court right now, so we'll see what he does with it. I told him you and I would be having a cup of tea after the boat pulls in. That gives him a little more time."

"What if he doesn't want to meet me?"

"Let's just see what happens. I gave him my card. He has my number."

Delaney can't help looking over her shoulder when she and Luella disembark and walk over to the coffee shop. She makes a point of choosing a chair that faces the doorway when they sit down. Luella orders a cup of chamomile tea claiming her nerves are rattled enough she doesn't need any caffeine. Delaney asks for a cup of regular coffee with a shot of espresso. She adds two sugars and keeps stirring long after the sugar would have dissolved.

"You're gonna whip that cup into a foamy frenzy if you don't stop stirring," Luella cautions. "Take a couple of deep breaths. I know it's hard but try to relax a bit if you can. It's only been five minutes since we got off the boat."

Delaney puts her stir stick on a napkin and watches the little whirlpool in her cup continue to spin. "I've got a nervous stomach, Luella. I think I need to go to the restroom. I'll be right back."

Luella goes over to a wicker basket and picks up a section of the *Chronicle*, then returns to her seat. She doesn't see Wade walk in the door. He pulls a third chair over to her table and looks around. Luella notices he's combed his hair and changed into a faded sport shirt and jeans.

"Oh, Mr. Tanner, I'm so glad you came," Luella says with a smile. "Delaney went to the Ladies'. She'll be back here in just a minute. Can I get you something to drink?"

"No, thank you Luella. I'll pass. I don't think they have anything here strong enough for a moment like this." He runs a hand through his hair. "Please call me Wade. May I ask how the two of you met?"

"The short version is that I lost a bracelet and she found it. Here she is now…"

Wade stands and turns. Delaney walks right up to him and extends her hand.

Luella sees she has managed to fix a smile on her face.

"Hi, I'm Delaney. Um, sorry. My hand is a little sweaty."

"Delaney. That's a pretty name. I have to tell you this was quite a surprise but a pleasant one. You can call me Wade."

They sit, and Delaney takes a swallow of her coffee, aware the cup seems to wobble a little in her hand. "Okay, this is kind of awkward," she says, putting her cup down. "I'm not sure who should start or where. Maybe I should go ahead?" She looks at Luella who gives her a smiling nod of encouragement.

"Brace yourself Wade, she might be a little over-caffein-ated," Luella says with a grin.

Delaney shifts in her seat. "Okay. This was a surprise to me, too. My mother always told me that you and your wife were killed in an automobile accident in Chicago right before I was born. So, obviously, that's not true."

Wade takes a deep breath. His face darkens. "It's such a long and complicated story Delaney. I'll see if I can make some sense out of it for you. Clearly, I owe you that much." He sits back in his seat and continues. "Your mother be-came pregnant in high school and as soon as your father, Marty, found out about it, he took off. I wanted to go after him because I thought he should accept the responsibility of fatherhood, but your mother wouldn't hear of it. Your grandmother, Doris, coddled your mother and even let her stay home from school because she didn't want her to suf-fer the stigma of an illegitimate pregnancy. I wasn't at all happy with that and we'd had quite a few arguments. Your mother was very manipulative and used to getting her own way. It was a rough Christmas that year. In fact, the holidays haven't been right for me ever since. Shortly after New Year's, I'd gone to bed upstairs but woke up hearing some sort of struggle going on."

"What do you mean about a struggle? Like someone fighting?" Delaney asks. She notices he has a pained, tired look on his face.

"I couldn't quite tell, Delaney. Seemed like banging around and raised voices. I was disoriented from sleep and by the time I got out of bed and opened my door, I could smell smoke. Elizabeth wasn't in her room and I couldn't find Doris. The smoke was thick downstairs and when I got outside, Elizabeth was there. She told the firemen she'd woken up, smelled smoke and ran out. The investigator's report said Doris died of smoke inhalation and the fire was likely caused by a frayed electrical cord igniting our Christmas tree. The Red Cross put Elizabeth and I into a temporary shelter." Wade lowers his head and continues, his voice shaky. "It was too much for me — losing my wife, my home. I couldn't handle it. I walked away from the shelter and left Elizabeth there. She was about a month or so away from her due date. She told me she was going to give the baby up for adoption and I figured the shelter people would put her in a home for unwed mothers. She wouldn't have wanted to be with me anyway and how could I have taken care of her if she did?" Wade pauses briefly and looks at Luella, as though expecting an answer. She shakes her head and he continues. "Later, I found out that Doris had changed her beneficiary on her life insurance policy to Elizabeth and Elizabeth collected that money a few months later when she turned eighteen. That's pretty much it, in a nutshell," Wade says. "I'm not proud of what I did, Delaney. I may as well have been dead."

Luella reaches over and puts her hand on his arm. "May I just say that I'm glad you're not and that you two have this opportunity to meet each other. From what I understand, life hasn't been easy for Delaney and what you've said explains a lot."

"Yeah. I finally moved out a little over a year ago to live on my own," Delaney adds. "It's a good thing I never had any sisters or brothers. She was a lousy single parent, always involved in one abusive relationship after another. Life was all about her, smoking dope and getting beat up."

Luella nods at Delaney, encouraging her to continue.

"I was told she had a bad fall recently and was in the hospital, so I went to see her yesterday. Her face is wrapped up in bandages and the minute she sees me she asks me to go down to the jail to see if I can bail out her most recent boyfriend. Seriously! I'm so done with her."

"Can't say I blame you. I'm so sorry," Wade says, dropping his gaze and shaking his head.

Despite her coffee with an extra shot, Delaney feels exhausted.

Luella finishes her tea and sets the empty cup on the table. An espresso machine hissing in the background suddenly stops, and the sound of a distant siren can be heard. She and Delaney hold each other with their eyes. The sound fades quickly.

"Well," Luella says, turning to Wade. "Where does this leave us?"

Wade clears his throat. "Delaney, may I have your telephone number? I'd like us to stay in touch."

"I'll trade you mine for yours," she says.

Numbers are written on corners torn from the newspaper and exchanged. Wade folds Delaney's number and slips it into his wallet.

They walk out of the coffee shop and stand by the fountain for a moment. Delaney shifts her weight from one foot to the other.

"I'll call you," Wade says. "That's a promise. We've got a lot of catching up to do."

Delaney's voice is caught in her throat, but she nods. He starts to extend his hand then puts his arm around her shoulders, giving her an awkward but gentle squeeze. Luella fishes a tissue out of her purse and blows her nose.

As she and Luella walk toward the parking lot, Delaney looks back over her shoulder. Wade is still standing by the fountain, his lunchbox at his feet. He waves at Delaney and she waves back.

Forty-Five

Delaney notices the lights are out at Murray's as Luella pulls into the driveway and parks. Standing next to the car, they embrace each other, neither wanting to be the first to let go. Delaney is the first to speak.

"Thank you isn't enough, Luella. I'm just blown away. I never would have even known I have a grandpa without your help. He's real now."

"He sure is and I'll bet he's thinking he made the right choice coming over to that coffee shop to meet you. I believe you and I came together for a reason and I'm glad I was able to help. You're gonna sleep good tonight, child. Your mind will be enjoying a well-deserved rest. Call me tomorrow afternoon and let me know how you're doing."

"I will. Good night Luella. Thank you so much for everything."

Not wanting to disturb Murray by using his phone to call Julian, Delaney lets herself in, brushes her teeth and climbs into bed fully clothed, barely managing to kick off her sandals before snuggling under her blanket.

Delaney tries to turn away from the sunlight filtering in through her window. She rubs her eyes and realizes it's almost 9:00 a.m. Yawning, she smiles to herself, remembering the events of yesterday. Before getting into the shower, she double-checks her purse to be sure she has Wade's number. After a quick bowl of cereal, Delaney goes next door to see Murray and call Julian.

Melody and Lyric are waiting on Murray's back step, anxious for their breakfast so Delaney puts a little food in their dishes. She smells coffee when she walks into the kitchen and notices the pot still seems to be full.

"Murray?" she calls. She looks in the store. It's not quite ten o'clock yet and he's not in there. She hadn't checked but she's sure his car is in the driveway. She hears a faint noise and listens again, carefully. It sounds like a weak groan. Delaney rushes to the bathroom.

"Murray! Oh my God!" Murray is on the floor, lying on his side, his arm across his chest clutching his shoulder.

Delaney runs into the kitchen and dials 9-1-1.

"Please! I need an ambulance fast! It's Murray Tompkins, Grass Roots Music. Hurry!" Delaney hangs up the phone while the dispatcher is still speaking, then runs to unlock the front door of the store and leave it open. She goes back to Murray and kneels on the floor next to him. He's still dressed in his pajamas. His eyes are open, and he blinks at her but can't seem to speak. His breath is coming in short, shallow pants.

"It's okay Murray, I'm right here," Delaney reassures him. "You're going to be fine. An ambulance will be here in a second. Hang on, Murray. Keep breathing okay? That's it. Hang on."

Delaney strokes his sweaty head. She hears a siren, faintly at first. Her own heart is pounding in her chest, but she knows she must get through this. She can't leave Murray. The siren grows louder, and Delaney looks down at him. He's still breathing, and his eyes are on her.

"It's okay, I'm not leaving you. We're both okay." She desperately wants to cover her ears but grasps his free hand instead, clenching her teeth. When she hears the paramedics coming up the steps, she yells out "Back here, in the bathroom!" Delaney climbs into Murray's bathtub to get out of their way. Two paramedics wearing rubber gloves are at his side in an instant. A third is standing in the hall, talking on his radio. It seems like it's only a matter of minutes before they have Murray strapped to a stretcher and loaded in the back of the ambulance. Delaney stands on the porch and watches the ambulance speed away, its siren blaring. When it turns the corner, she goes back inside, takes a piece of paper and writes:

"SORRY. CLOSED TODAY. EMERGENCY"

and tapes it to the front door. She locks the door and goes into the kitchen to call Julian. As soon as she hears his voice, she bursts into tears.

"Delaney? Are you okay? Baby, what's the matter?"

"They just took Murray away in an ambulance," she cries.

"I'm going to borrow a car and I'll be right over," he says. "Stay put, babe."

Delaney grabs a fistful of tissues and drops into a chair.

Julian arrives a few minutes later and finds Delaney pacing on the sidewalk, waiting for him. She jumps in the car and they head for the nearest hospital in Vallejo.

"He can't die Julian! I think it was a heart attack. The paramedics put stickers and wires on his chest. Can you go a little faster? Please?"

"We're almost there. A couple more blocks," Julian says, racing through a yellow light.

A security guard at the reception desk tells them he doesn't have a "Murray Tompkins" listed as a patient but asks them to wait a moment. He picks up a phone and dials a four-digit number, turning to put his back to Julian and Delaney so they can't hear his part of the conversation. A moment later, he hangs up.

"Apparently Mr. Tompkins was admitted through the emergency room and has been taken to surgery. The surgery waiting area is on the second floor." He points to an elevator across the lobby. Delaney grabs Julian's hand and thanks the guard. Upstairs in the waiting room, a volunteer greets them. She tells them a surgery nurse will come by as soon as there is something to report. They are welcome to help themselves to coffee or tea from a cart in the corner. She disappears, carrying an armload of magazines.

Delaney picks up a travel magazine and turns the pages without even looking at it. Julian watches the news on an overhead television screen. She puts the magazine down and begins to pace. Julian gets up and puts his arm around her. He leads her back to a seat.

"All we can do is wait. It's out of our hands." He speaks to her softly and she looks at him, her eyes filled with tears. He pulls a tissue from the box on the table and hands it to her.

"Do you realize what you did, Delaney?" he asks. She shakes her head. "You probably saved his life. That's huge! If it hadn't been for you, he wouldn't be here right now. Don't you see?" He touches her chin, looks into her eyes and pulls her close to him. They sit close together, Julian with his arm around Delaney, for the better part of an hour before a nurse appears in the doorway.

"Are you family members of Mr. Tompkins?" she asks.

Delaney immediately stands up. "I'm his neighbor and his friend. I called the ambulance. Murray only has his sister and she lives in Minneapolis. Is he doing alright?"

The nurse smiles. "He's certainly doing much better. The doctor cleared a blockage in his artery and placed a stent. Mr. Tompkins will be in recovery for a little while and then he'll be moved to a room on this floor." The nurse looks at the clock on the wall. "I'd say by the time you two go have some lunch and come back; he might be ready for a very brief visit. Don't rush. Let's give him until about three o'clock or so, alright?"

Delaney blinks back tears as she nods. Julian thanks the nurse and walks Delaney to the elevator. Despite his assurances they have plenty of time, she doesn't want to leave the hospital.

"Personally, I think a hero deserves something better than cafeteria food but it's your choice," he says with a grin.

They find the cafeteria, grab trays and get in line behind a mix of visitors and hospital staff in scrubs. Delaney chooses a large salad from the cooler and Julian asks for a burger and fries. He fills their plastic glasses at the soda machine, and they sit at a table by a window that looks out on the "Remembrance Garden."

"I'm so glad he's going to be okay. I've never been that scared in my whole life. Did I even thank you for coming to get me?" Delaney asks, opening a packet of dressing. "What time do you have to have your friend's car back?"

"No worries. He doesn't need it until late this afternoon so we're good. Hey, tell me about what happened yesterday." Julian takes a bite of his burger and juice dribbles down his chin.

Delaney reaches over with her napkin and wipes it for him, smiling. She tells him about the night at Luella's and the trip on the ferry to the city.

"Luella sounds like an amazing lady," he says, sipping his soda. "I'd like to meet her."

"You will, Julian and you'll like her." Delaney proceeds to tell him about finally meeting her grandfather in the coffee shop and what that was like. She notices he's stopped eating and is listening intently to her story. She takes one of his fries and nibbles on it.

"So, that's pretty much it. Cool, huh? By the time I got back last night it was too late to call you. In fact, that's why I went over to Murray's this morning. I guess it's a good thing it turned out that way."

After stacking their trays, Julian suggests a walk outside in the fresh air of the garden. They hold hands as they follow the meandering path in and out of sunlight and shadow, admiring the plants and flowers.

"This is such a peaceful place," Delaney says, pausing for a moment.

"I think that's the point," Julian says, grinning.

Delaney checks her watch. "It's after two o'clock, Julian. Let's go back in. I need to use the restroom before we go back upstairs."

"Good idea."

They stop at the reception desk again and this time they're given a room number on the second floor. Riding up in the elevator alone, Delaney squeezes Julian's hand and he gives her a quick kiss. She blushes and smiles. The door opens.

"I'll hang out in the waiting room while you visit," Julian says.

"I don't think I'll be too long," Delaney replies, aware of a sense of déjà vu as she recalls the same scene from another hospital a couple of days before. She stops at the nurses' station first to be sure it's alright to go to Murray's room.

The nurse looks up from her paperwork. "Are you Delaney?"

"Yes, I am."

"Please go ahead in," she says, pointing to his room. "He's groggy but he's been asking for you."

Delaney smiles as she thanks her and walks across the hall.

Murray is propped up in the bed, connected to several blinking monitors and an IV pole. She notices he's pale and seems half awake. As soon as he sees her, his face brightens. He lifts his hand with effort. Delaney takes it, and leaning carefully over his railing, kisses him lightly on the forehead.

"I think I like your regular pajamas better," she says, looking at his disheveled gown.

"You saved my life sweetheart," he replies, his voice barely above a whisper.

"I was just returning the favor, Murray." Delaney wipes a tear away from her cheek with her sleeve. "I want you to rest and not worry about anything at the store. I'll reopen tomorrow morning. I'm so glad you're going to be okay."

Delaney notices his eyelids are drooping as though he wants to sleep. She gently lays his hand down on the bed and steps away. When he appears to be sleeping comfortably, she quietly walks out of the room.

Back at the nurse's station, Delaney asks the nurse to write Murray's telephone number on his chart and tells the nurse this is the best way to reach her.

When Delaney returns to the waiting room, she sees Julian sitting there, holding a bouquet of flowers. "These are for you," he says, handing them to her.

She wraps her arms around his neck and hugs him. "He's going to be okay, Julian. I'm so happy!" Delaney sniffs the flowers and smiles. "This is the absolute best day of my life!"

"He's lucky to have you. So am I."

Julian pulls up in front of Grass Roots.

"Damn. Wish I could spend the rest of the day with you. Gotta get this car back and go to work though. I'll come by in the morning."

Delaney turns to Julian and kisses him tenderly.

"Thank you for the ride, the flowers and especially for being there when I needed you." She steps out of the car and closes the door. "See you in the morning!"

As she unlocks her door, Lyric dashes over and puts his paws up on her planter box. She wonders if he's just stretching or trying to show her the first, red, ripe cherry tomato.

Acknowledgements

First and foremost, my deepest gratitude goes to my husband Duane for his steady support and encouragement throughout the writing of this book and to our youngest son, Mark, who innocently planted the tiny seed that inspired this story when he was two months old.

Heartfelt thanks go to readers of my first draft: Gloria Colter, Pat Tyler, Janet Snyder, Angel Vion and McKaley Phillips for their comments and suggestions, particularly to Pat for her early editorial-level review of a revised draft.

The revised manuscript was critiqued by a dedicated group of fellow Redwood Writers members: Karen Hart, Mary Lynn Archibald, David Sydney Scott and Jean Wong who each offered invaluable feedback, chapter by chapter.

I wish to also express my appreciation to members of my longtime writing group dubbed "The Feisties" (also known as "Wise Women of the Pen") for their comments on portions of the story that I felt needed additional input.

I am sincerely grateful also, to Marlene Cullen and Armando García-Dávila, who generously gave of their time and offered helpful advice.

Finally, if not for the expert assistance of Jo-Anne Rosen of Wordrunner Press in readying the manuscript for publication and Stefanie Fontecha at beetiful.com for translating my ideas for a cover into a beautiful, enduring design, this book would never have taken root.

About the Author

As a writer, Brenda strives to gently tug one strand of the web that connects us all. She is inspired by nature and the human experience. Her years as a courtroom clerk and high school secretary have no doubt exerted some influence over her writing.

As a reader, the books that have stayed with her are those she was slow to finish — not wanting the stories to end.

This is Brenda's first novel, conceived and hatched on an old chicken farm in Northern California where she and her husband raised their four adult sons.

Her work has appeared in *Small Farmer's Journal, Mom Egg Review, Persimmon Tree, THEMA*, the California Writers Club *Literary Review*, and in various anthologies. She has been honored with first place awards for non-fiction and flash fiction at the Mendocino Coast and Central Coast Writers Conferences, respectively.

Made in the USA
San Bernardino, CA
19 July 2020